AS MAX SAW IT

As Max Saw It

LOUIS BEGLEY

ALFRED A. KNOPF · NEW YORK · 1994

THIS IS A BORZOI BOOK
PUBLISHED BY ALFRED A. KNOPF, INC.

Library of Congress Cataloging-in-Publication Data
Begley, Louis.
  As Max saw it / Louis Begley
     p.   cm.
  ISBN 0-679-43307-4
  1. Law teachers—Fiction.   2. Architects—Fiction.
3. Friendship—Fiction.   I. Title.
PS3552.E373A9   1994
813´.54—dc20

                                      93-45788
                                        CIP

Manufactured in the United States of America
Published April 18, 1994
Reprinted Once
Third Printing, July 1994

To strike his living hi and ho,
To tick it, tock it, turn it true . . .
        —WALLACE STEVENS,
          "The Man with the Blue Guitar"

AS MAX SAW IT

I

L A RUMOROSA, for that was the name of the Joyce villa
on the promontory just below Bellagio, where Lake
Como divides to form a pair of clown's pantaloons,
blue and green, gold speckled and shimmering, was one of
those places where, sooner or later, everyone stayed. My
turn came in a manner I greeted with a mixture of gratitude
and resignation; it was like other invitations to grand houses
or elegant lunches and dinners of which I had recently been
the object: the hostess had authorized a real guest, her intimate friend, to bring me along. Relationships did not stick to
me. Although Edna had known me really quite well—she
and her best friend, Janie, had been the most spectacular ex-
amples of a new species of Radcliffe girl that appeared,
miraculously, out of the Midwest in the fall of my last year at
college, all patently rich and tall, and so beautifully formed,
their bosoms beckoning under angora sweaters the shades of
which matched the subtle hues of their lipstick, that I had felt
moved, against all dictates of good sense (I was conducting
with a much plainer, but sexy and freckled, graduate student
an affair that was to endure until Easter vacation of the year
in which this narrative opens, and besides, quite clearly, I was
not their sort), to attempt to flirt at first with her and later

with Janie—she had not telephoned or written to signify that she expected my arrival. Instead, after Arthur and I, guided by an inadequately shaved man in a striped vest with brass buttons, at last found her on the eastern terrace of the villa, which was shaded against the postprandial sun by the building itself, she let out squeals so enthusiastic, calling me alternately her *bébé* and her old beau, that, if I had not known better, I might have believed, at least for a moment, that the idea of having me there had been her own. To the left and right stretched the formal flower gardens. Directly below, at the end of a white alley bordered by marble sculptures and benches, was the celebrated flowering-laurel maze, its symmetry mystifying even from this privileged vantage point. The group of guests displayed on armchairs, poufs, and chaise longues, drinking coffee and smoking, seemed no more penetrable. Arthur knew them all, and I was variously introduced as his or Edna's friend to deeply bronzed figures in white cotton or silk, from whose feet dangled sandals sustained by an insouciant but perfect toe—or equally white loafers with metal decorations attesting to their provenance.

I recognized Charlie Swan, unmistakable because of his extraordinary height and tightly curled hair cut very short, so that his head reminded one of a Roman bust—and was relieved that he too knew me instantly. Noted for his prowess in a single scull and with a martini shaker, my classmate at college although he was some four years older, it was believed, I remembered distinctly, that he had obtained Janie's ultimate favors and enjoyed them at least until her graduation from college—although he and I both graduated at the end of her freshman year. Such long tenure had been made possible by Charlie's having stayed on in Cambridge, to study architecture, when most of us departed for military service. He had already served, in Korea, before going to college. What happened between them later I didn't know, but I had heard that Janie had gone from one marriage with a stockbroker to another, and then possibly to a third, and was living in Chicago. Charlie had also married, someone I met briefly at one of the parties that followed their engagement, and then possibly at a college reunion, whose image—as I had retained it—did not seem to fit any of the women on the terrace. He had also become famous; more so, I think, than any other member of our class. An entire waterfront development in Hamburg bore his name, which was nice, given the aquatic association. He was responsible for the best new skyscraper in downtown Houston. Beach houses designed by him appeared regularly in *Vogue* essays on the habits and habitats of Hampton millionaires.

But I did not know Rodney Joyce, and it was time I met him. Edna led me to him: Here is Max, my lost baby.

Her husband inspected me with apparent benevolence.

I will be going to Torno, he announced, down the shore, a little after five when the shops reopen, to pick up a gadget for the launch.

Then, squeezing my left elbow even as he continued to shake my hand, he added, as though to demonstrate he knew who I was: Relics from Edna's past interest me. She is such a collector! Will you come to the village with me? There is plenty of time for you to swim first, if that's what you like. Pool, or lake from the boathouse.

★ ★ ★

HE HANDLED THE LARGE CAR with a sort of skilled indolence, indifferent to horns, blinking headlights, and drivers accelerating past us on the two-lane road. There were sights he wanted me to note, like the Rockefeller establishment right nearby, which was in fact worth a visit, and bits of local history. No trouble at all; the director would be pleased to meet a fellow academic. Edna and he might get him to come over for dinner. The Rumorosa had been theirs for more than ten years; Edna bought it—with her own money, he was careful to mention, because it had been her idea—a year or so after he retired from the foreign service.

His last post had been in Paris—a political counselor. They decided to remain, and were still living in the same apartment, on the Faubourg Saint-Honoré, which was not long on charm, but extremely comfortable and, in their case, because the windows all gave onto gardens, quiet as a tomb. Obviously, living in Paris and having that position, which encouraged one to get around, had made Northern Italy their backyard. They had actually been invited to seminars in the Rockefeller establishment. On the other side of the lake stood the smaller but infinitely more beautiful villa of our mutual New York friends—he made the obligatory joke or two about them—and they had also stayed there, both as guests and as lodgers.

During one of those sojourns they happened to go across the water in a gondola for lunch at the Rumorosa, which they found to be the best house on the lake and the most lovable house they had seen anywhere. When the Ognissanti scandal broke, Edna got on the phone to the family's lawyers in Milan within a week. She sensed that there would be a need to raise cash quickly, and she was right. She was able to buy the villa complete with everything from table linen all the way to the boat whose motor had just conked out. And the servants remained, contentedly it would seem, as there had been no defections.

I knew enough from Arthur's remarks and gossip about the Joyces in the houses Arthur and I had visited on our way to the Rumorosa to add some color to that sketch. The last embassy job, as indeed all of Rodney's employments since he first came to Paris after the war to work with the Marshall Plan people, had more to do with the agency in Virginia than with conventional diplomacy. His qualifications for whatever it was he really did were manifold: a Silver Star war record, friendships with the right fellow Yalies, a gift for European languages, and an inconspicuous but ample personal fortune that required no attention from him whatsoever. It derived from manufacturing activities centered around Akron, Ohio, and was locked up in trust. That he had married Edna was less of a chance event than most marriages even in those days. Edna was from the same suburb of Akron; her family were friends of the senior Joyces. Already as a little girl she had understood that Rodney was Prince Charming. The other side of the coin was the limitation of his perfectly serviceable intelligence. It took him only so far, not far enough to become a master puppeteer, for instance, deputy director. He could not even aspire to a job in the White House or its security annex that fit his social position. Hence the onset of a form of laziness—doubtless favored by the childless, gregarious luxury in which he and Edna lived—and his early retirement.

The spare part for the motor was ready and waiting. Rodney examined it with evident understanding, and remembered that he also needed varnish and steel wool. We looked at a Bombard. Rodney said it was too large; the owner of the water garage undertook to check in Como on the availability and price of something more like a dinghy. Then Rodney proposed a drink in the café on the square.

What about Charlie? I asked. Is his wife—I'm no longer sure of her name—is she also here?

That's old business. Charlie's frying other fish now. You will see.

We finished our second round of Punt e Mes and climbed into Rodney's Citroën.

And you? he asked. I only know that at college everybody was afraid of you because you had all the answers, and that you became a law school professor!

He turned out to be a good interrogator. Genuine interest or professional habit? I couldn't be sure. But as we continued our stately progress toward the Rumorosa, Rodney luxuriating in the leather comfort of his seat, I told him how, after college—where I surely had terrified no one, least of all Edna and her glamorous friends—and service in the peacetime army, I did return to the Law School in Cambridge. Then one thing led to another: good grades led to the *Review*, good grades sustained even after that elevation led to more concentrated benevolence on the part of two of the great men who were my teachers, their favor led to the right clerkships, and from there it was but a hop, skip, and a jump to a junior faculty appointment, which turned rather quickly into my present position.

What exactly do you teach?

Contracts, and some legal history. You see, I am curious about obligations.

Then I added, perhaps because I feared he was losing interest: Not having a respectful attitude toward making money was a help throughout. If you wish to call it help! Anyway, that's how I slipped into my marginal form of existence.

You can't call being friends with Arthur marginal! He raves about you. What's the connection there? He has nothing to do with Harvard.

I explained: In fact he is in Cambridge a good deal, because of a company on Route 128 he has put money into. It has a Business School affiliation. I met him at a colleague's, at dinner, and we fell to talking. Later, he came to dinner with me and a woman I was then living with. I introduced him to some of the more interesting types among the reigning Brahmins, the ones he especially wanted to know. He was a hit and we became friends. Now I depend on him for my vacations.

You could do worse!

I agreed, and kept on talking.

THAT NIGHT, in my room, listening to the radio, I heard Nixon resign. It was difficult to make out his words through RAI's voice-over translation. I had been waiting for this moment, but the satisfaction I had expected from the ogre's disgrace somehow eluded me. Did he feel shame, I wondered, uttering all these words that explained nothing? I was not satisfied with myself either. Why had I been so assiduous in my replies to Rodney, almost fawning? What business of his was it after how many years of a neatly shared existence Kate had chosen to leave me for her newly appointed colleague in the Slavic studies department? Presumably, at that point, Rodney was no longer paying attention, so that my elegy on afternoons in the Widener and evenings at Cronin's did not run a serious risk of being repeated for the amusement of Edna. Besides, would I not recite it for her as well, at the drop of a hint of curiosity, throwing in even the more sordid details? For instance, my bitterness at the loss of the use of Kate's house in the meadow above White River Junction, which had turned me into a summer nomad without hearth or home; the small victory she obtained when I signed over my white VW with a brand-new sunroof, after she confronted me with the irrebuttable argument that she would need it to go back and forth between Cambridge and Vermont, whereas I wouldn't; my own larger victory, won when I kept the apartment on Sparks Street. Nixon and Max— some team! If pressed, I would even have told her that ultimately it was the faint indignity of being the abandoned party, and the inconvenience, I minded the most. Kate's skin had begun to coarsen; she was smoking too much; and she had become shrill. In time, I might do better.

THE JOYCES were conscientious hosts. The next morning there was an organized departure for Como, to visit the Duomo and also Sant'Abbondio, which they considered possibly more important. When I came down to the drive, jittery from sleeplessness, the first observations on the cataclysm that had just taken place must have already been exchanged. Arthur, who professed to admire Nixon and Kissinger for being such shits, was already in Edna's two-seater. He would find in her a suitable midwestern audience. I waved to Charlie; he waved back as he got into the last available seat in a car apparently belonging to a woman with red hair in a khaki jumpsuit, whom I took to be Italian. Rodney may have gone ahead; in any case he wasn't there to help the dwindling group of guests sort themselves out. Should I get the Fiat Arthur and I had rented at the Milan airport? I could see that some cars were not full, but how was I to know whether their empty seats weren't spoken for? I felt the onset of a familiar mixture of awkwardness and irritation—it was like standing with a plate and glass in one's hands at a buffet in a room where everyone else seems to have a place by prearrangement, so that one's choice is between sitting down alone, perhaps next to the telephone, or dragging a chair over to a table surrounded by animated diners—all quite fond of one another—in the hope that they will open a space for the embarrassed stranger. I thought I would just miss this trip. Exaggerating the gesture, I slapped my forehead with my hand, as though I had, all of a sudden, remembered something important, and ran back into the house.

The swimming pool, I had been told, was on the other side of the maze. I made my way there through thick smells of colorful borders and bushes in full bloom. The pool turned out to be oval, lined with white marble—no other material had currency at the Rumorosa—and surrounded at a distance by a circle of slender cypresses. At its edge, legs in the water, face concentrated over a backgammon board, sat a figure of such startlingly perfect beauty that I thought it was a girl—not seen at dinner the night before because she was too young or because she was only an employee at the villa—now taking advantage of the quiet that had fallen upon the surroundings to sun herself without her bikini top. When I came closer, close enough for the figure to sense my presence and turn to look in my direction, I saw that I was wrong: it was Eros himself, longhaired and dimpled, his skin the color of pale amber, for it had pleased the boy god to wash off the matte finish of white powder under which, day after day, he allowed himself to be admired, disguised as a statue, on the pedestal at the end of the villa's central alley.

He smiled, put on his dark glasses, and spoke to me in English: I guess the bus for Como has left. My name is Toby. Why did you stay behind?

I told him my name and that I had no real excuse; possibly I hadn't wanted to get into a car in which there was no one I knew and hear stuff about Nixon I might not agree with.

I understand that.

Why weren't you at dinner last night?

Reasons something like yours for not going to Como, and that's why I didn't go to Como either. Do you want a game?

He added, Nixon was once my dad's lawyer, but I don't know about American politics.

I told him I had never played backgammon.

He smiled again and said, It's not hard, I'll teach you.

He must have given such lessons many times. My inability to count spaces at a glance provoked in him tolerant amusement. He did not need to count at all. The small rapacious hand skimmed over the board moving his own men and, when I made mistakes, mine as well, stacking them up in neat piles and, without a pause, setting up a new game each time he won.

We should play for money, he ventured. Small stakes and a handicap for you. It will force you to pay attention.

I assured him my problem was not with concentration but arithmetic, and the will to win.

That amused him.

Charlie said you're a law professor. Don't they all know how to count?

Almost all.

We played a few more times, enough to let him conclude I had grasped the principles but would never be an interesting adversary. Then he put away the set, ran to the diving board, rose from it like a tawny bird, descended, and swam so fast and so beautifully that out of respect I remained at the pool's edge, although, after so much sun, I too wanted to jump in. He understood, and stopping at the near end of the pool, called out, Come on, Professor Max, don't worry about keeping up! You can't. I've been in competitions since I was a kid.

I obeyed, and as I swam back and forth in my plodding fashion, keeping well to the side, my curiosity about this strange, beautiful boy—he could hardly be more than sixteen—kept growing. He had the grace and easy kindness of a young prince. Was he one? The English he spoke was perfect, but it wasn't necessarily American or British. No American boy I had ever met possessed such a manner.

When we had dried off and sat down in the shade of a

Roman umbrella, he explained, just as naturally as he had imparted to me the basic rules of backgammon, that he was on vacation from a boarding school near Lausanne, where his father had dropped him off—these were the words he used—three years earlier, after he and his mother divorced. He was the only child. The father went back to Beirut and his trading business with Saudi Arabia; the mother was in America, in a hospital.

She's crazy, you see. It began a couple of years before I went to Lausanne. She wouldn't leave her room. Then one night she jumped out of the window. She hit the roof of the greenhouse and got pretty badly cut.

I said that was horrible. He agreed. Then he smiled, making me wonder whether some of his cheerfulness wasn't a series of nervous tics, like dance steps someone might execute for no reason.

What about now? I asked him. Why are you here?

He smiled again.

Charlie brought me. I work for him, at his firm's Geneva office. My dad got me the job. Dad knows Rodney Joyce too. They were spooks together after the war. It's my summer training.

LATER THAT DAY, during the long melancholy interval between the real and official end of an August afternoon, when at dusk *la mosca cede a la zanzara* and drinks are served, I wandered out to the front of the villa with a book, thinking I would read in the last of the sun. There was no sound except for the back and forth ping of a tennis ball. I guessed it was Rodney playing singles with some carefully chosen guest, perhaps Arthur, since Arthur had not opened when I knocked on the door of his room. One imagined siestas in shuttered bedrooms, then somewhat later tubs redolent of the expensive bath oils supplied by Edna, and women beginning to wonder how they would dress for dinner. I had expected to be alone, but there, like a beached whale on a wicker settee, a glass of white wine in hand, a bottle in a bucket of ice beside him, was Charlie. I saw him before he noticed me. He had no book or magazine; his eyes were fixed on the lake below us, perhaps on a boat making its way toward Dongo or Gravedona. When I said his name, he rose to greet me with a sort of abbreviated bear hug, then pressed me down into the other corner of the settee. Encased in white linen, his bulk struck me as prodigious. It wasn't a former athlete's fat; during the momentary embrace, I felt that his body was as hard as it seemed heavy. Perhaps my memory of him was faulty, perhaps time had playfully doubled his size. He poured a glass of wine, handed it to me, and attacked.

I am surprised to see that you and Arthur travel around together. What a way to come to this place! Don't you realize he is known everywhere as a snob and a rotter? You used to be an intellectual, someone really serious. What's happened to you?

I haven't changed in that respect; that may be why I wouldn't be here at all if Arthur hadn't brought me. Why pick on him? Isn't everybody here a snob? You and the Joyces, for instance? And what do you mean by calling him a rotter?

Just that. You are out of your depth with him. He is spoiled to the core. His business deals are sharp, he squeezes his partners, all he cares about is being invited to places like this, and getting his name into gossip columns.

Have you done business with him?

Certainly not! My work is making sublime buildings, and they don't come cheap, and they are not for common speculators. Your new pal has no use for anything that's of good quality, never mind great art. It's instinctive. He thinks quality is for suckers who subscribe to that magazine he publishes, which I use for toilet paper!

He added sadly, You shouldn't allow yourself to be seen with him.

There are people one knows for long periods of time without any element of choice having entered into the matter. They pop up regularly in a defined context; when at some point they disappear, one doesn't miss them. So far as I was concerned, Charlie belonged in that category. That he should take upon himself to be intrusive, and so harsh about Arthur, was outrageous. Whatever my own views about my traveling companion might be, and the foundations on which our relations reposed, I could think of no reason why Charlie should doubt that Arthur and I were friends. I had no doubt whatsoever that at the Rumorosa he was my real host. I told Charlie I found the prospect of continuing our conversation unpleasant and stood up to leave.

Charlie seized my hand. He had tiny feet but his hands were huge, as if made to grasp oars, in scale with the rest of him.

Don't take offense. I have spoken with too much feeling, but there is a reason. Let's walk toward the lake. I will explain. There may not be another opportunity.

I found it difficult to refuse, and, to a degree, I wanted to know what he would say. We followed a path through a cypress grove to yet another terrace that ended at the edge of the water in a balustrade. On it, facing the lake, stood a row of Olympians, among them Hermes and Hercules and, next to the latter, perhaps by chance and perhaps because the patron who had commissioned this display enjoyed small ironies of the gods' family relations, Ganymede. Meanwhile Charlie talked.

You didn't attend my wedding even though I invited that hairy-legged graduate student you were so inappropriately associated with. Perhaps you still are! That was a painful surprise for me, and for Diane too. You paid little attention, you have probably forgotten the effort I made to make sure that you met Diane immediately after our engagement. As soon as I learned that you would be in New York, I prevailed on her cousin Anson to include you in the party he gave for Diane; you and she hit it off at once; I had counted on that and asked you to dinner with us afterward at Giovanni's. You declined, without a reason. That was a sign I failed to read, because as I said your brutality in not coming to the wedding, which was really very small, very intimate, considering how large Diane's and my families are, took us by surprise. You hurt me very deeply.

For God's sake, Charlie, that was more than ten years ago! I meant no harm. Didn't I write that I was sorry? What's the connection between these imagined slights and poor Arthur?

I did receive a sort of form letter—typed!—about a problem with your car. Perfect nonsense, you could have taken the train. And you sealed that expression of contempt by your wedding present—a majolica cachepot! Could one send such a thing to me! I smashed it at once.

Had Charlie become insane? He advanced upon me with such ferocity that I found myself cornered, my back against the balustrade, on my right a monumental flowerpot planted with white geraniums. In the meantime, I had managed to recollect why I had so "brutally" skipped Charlie and Diane's wedding. Kate and I had in fact come to New York, a friend of Kate's being providentially absent so that we could spend the weekend in her apartment, with the firm intention of driving on Saturday after lunch to Short Hills, where the reception was to be held on the estate belonging to Diane's grandparents. We had been told that the place resembled a game reserve, and we wanted to see it. At the time, though, my sexual obsession with Kate was at its height. We didn't go out to lunch, made love instead on the friend's Murphy bed, and fell sound asleep. By the time we awakened, it was possible, but not certain, that we could reach on time that—for us—obscure part of New Jersey. Rather than taking the chance, I made tuna-fish sandwiches, which we ate in bed, and, thus strengthened, we resumed our activities. I may have suggested to Kate that we dedicate them as an epithalamium to the happy couple.

I did not think this ampler explanation would appease Charlie; besides, whatever might be the cause of his bizarre upset and resentment, I was not sure I wanted to make him feel better. The remark about Kate's legs was a further outrage, even if I had also deplored her refusal—temporary as it turned out—to work against nature's design with a safety razor or a hair remover.

It has everything to do with Arthur, and your being here under his dishonoring auspices, he resumed. I rejoiced when Edna told me I would see you. Of course, she had the good taste and savoir faire not to reveal with whom! I might have vomited. In that past, which to you seems so dim, I elected you in petto, because I alone could see inside you something strong and hard that someday would be revealed in great glory, just as what I had hidden inside me has been revealed. For others—particularly Janie and Edna—you were just another pretentious little poseur wrapped around some tutor sipping tea at the Signet! Yes, I elected you in secret to be my secret friend. That was a gift of myself. Now perhaps you can understand my disappointment, no, bitter humiliation to see that you are still the sycophant!

Had he not been so large and manifestly powerful, I would surely have hit him with one of Edna's green metal chairs, which were conveniently placed nearby. Instead, unaccountably, with my right hand I clawed the soil inside the flowerpot. It was very wet; the gardener must have watered it that same afternoon. I took a fistful of the stuff and threw it at Charlie, aiming at his face. It landed at the level of his breast pocket, making a large, dripping stain. I continued to bombard him while he stared with his mouth wide open. Then, just as unaccountably, we both began to laugh, unable to stop, until tears ran down our cheeks. Quite exhausted, I undertook, as a token of reconciliation, to pat him on the shoulder, and left a long streak of dirt on his sleeve.

All right, he said, that's enough. You haven't turned out badly after all.

He sat down on one of the chairs I had contemplated braining him with, took out his pocket handkerchief, and thoughtfully brushed his suit.

This will dry quite nicely, but I will get into something else when we go back to the house, he announced. Look, he pointed to the lake, we are at the confines of the ancient world. The villa of Pliny the Younger stands on the other shore. To your right, the murderous Alps. Greek gods guarding against Hannibal's elephants. Here, vineyards, apiaries, sheep peacefully grazing in the meadows. Paradise for the learned and sensitive of heart. In me, everything has changed since those days when you took so little trouble to know me. I have been very lonely.

I began to mumble something about having heard that he had divorced Diane. Immediately, he interrupted me.

Preordained passion and resurrection. My true work as an artist and a man began at that moment. Someday, you will see the best of what I have done. I will explain the unifying, directing thought, and you will grasp it, because you are sensitive and intelligent. Henceforth, you are one of my intimates—they are very few! Stay with me when you wish. If you like France, I have a house in Vézelay almost as ancient as the basilica. I am building a nest in the trees above Rio. My apartment in New York is in the River House. I will send you a key and give instructions that you are to be admitted whenever you choose. This morning you met my young employee. Children and small animals are the best

judges of character. He spoke well of you. Do not betray me
again!

Before I could reply, he offered me a cigar, clipped its end,
helped me light it, lit one himself, put his arm through mine,
and pulled me at a rapid pace toward the villa.

AFTER MY BATH, I looked for Arthur again in his room.
Once more, he wasn't there. I found him downstairs, on the
eastern terrace where our visit to the Rumorosa had begun.
The villa was narrow and long—the living room and the
gallery on the ground floor occupied its entire width—so
that one seemed always to be going from one side of the
house to the other. Rodney and Edna and the woman with
red hair were there too. I sat down with them. The setting
sun had filled the villa and made its windows glimmer like
the lake's water in the gentle ocher and yellow facade. Here
the light was gray and cold.

Rodney told me to make myself a whiskey. Arthur and he
were still in tennis clothes. He had beaten Arthur in the last
set and continued the analysis of tennis such as it had been
taught to him: strong service and reliable, accurate baseline
play.

You fellows are getting to be as old as me, catching up, he
told Arthur. Every time you rushed to the net I got you.

I am off my game. I should only stay in houses where I can
play. Please talk Laura into building a court or cutting down
on her hospitality. She has invited me to Belluno for a week.
I can't resist the best wine and peasant food in Italy, but there
won't be any tennis. By the way, Max, you are coming too!

So the red hair was called Laura. She addressed me. In a tenor voice, speaking rapid accented English, she assured me she absolutely counted on me; otherwise Arthur might not come, and she wanted Arthur to see some graphics that were just right for his office in Milan—in fact for any office. Did I have an office, she inquired. She would have things in Belluno, of course, but if I was still in Italy in September I might want to visit the gallery. To prevent my evident confusions getting the better of me, Edna informed me lazily from her couch that Laura's gallery was in Milan; she sold fabulous new work.

I was finding Laura attractive. Matter-of-fact, lively, and pleasant, without a hint of coiled-up aggressions that might be released at any moment, and so elegantly cared for—women like her did not turn up at the Cambridge dinner parties to which I was invited. I observed her varnished toenails. Wondering whether there was a link between Arthur and her, I said that my room in Langdell, at the Law School, could use something bright, and that if the invitation was for a date before I had to start teaching I would like to accept.

There is no problem, we will go to Laura's straight from here, declared Arthur. It's a pleasant day's drive. You can go in Laura's car and I'll follow. We'll stop for lunch at Giancarlo and Bettina's.

Thus the next *étape* of my journey in Italy was settled. I experienced a strange mixture of well-being and light-headedness, assisted, I supposed, by the large dose of whiskey I had poured into my glass. Somehow, from the world of those little hotels Kate culled in her library of Fodor's guides and magazine clippings, to which we would rush in fear of losing our reservation, establishments where the room with beams and provincial furniture would turn out to have squashed mosquito stains on the wallpaper and a bed that squeaked, I had penetrated into a magical realm of cashless bounty and comfort. It was odd to think that neither Laura nor the Joyces seemed to find my presence within it a jarring surprise; if that impression was correct, why had I been kept out until this moment? Arthur must have said Open Sesame on my behalf. Could someone else have done it, or was it necessary that the revolution of Fortune's wheel bring about a unique confluence of persons and time? And who had opened the gates for him, or the red-haired Laura? It was possible, it occurred to me, that I was naively mistaking cheerful good manners for gold, and would need to hurry to catch the train from Belluno to Milan and to my plane back to Boston before my visit became an embarrassment. I decided to repress that small-town New England suspicion. Edna slapped at a mosquito and announced that we should go in until the wind from the lake rose—which it would, conveniently, just before dinner.

As Arthur was about to follow the others, who were going up to change, I asked if he would stay a moment longer and talk with me.

Gladly, he replied. Let's sit down in the living room. We'll have it to ourselves.

I told him first that it had occurred to me I would be wrong to go to Belluno. Wouldn't he rather be alone with Laura—what was the point of having an extra man in that sort of situation?

Arthur laughed.

It's not even a situation. Besides, between now and the time we arrive there, Laura will have invited ten other people. It's a big house: beautiful but run-down and informal, not like here. Real Italy—you will love it! She'll be disappointed if you refuse. In Italy, law professors teach maybe once a week. They're more like important lawyers; they give legal advice. Laura has little businesses in many places, a bit of money here and a bit there. Since you are a professor, she figures that if you come to her house as a guest she can ask you for free advice—probably about taxes! Anyway, where is the harm? She seems to like you.

So there was no attachment between them. I felt a flash of desire and hope and thought that they too had better be repressed before I made a fool of myself.

What about Charlie, I asked. How well do you know him? I hadn't realized you knew him at all.

Why? Has he been talking to you about me? I bet he tried to blacken my name.

He certainly has some strong feelings.

He's got them about everything—especially winning prizes! You know our company has an investment in *Città*. Each year the magazine gives prizes for the five best new buildings. They are reviewed in the fall issue, with expensive photographs, essays by well-known critics—the works!— and then *Città* sponsors a scholarly exhibition at the MoMA and in Stuttgart. The thing started as a nice little routine, but now it's considered a big deal. The editors propose the buildings, but the winners are picked by an outside jury. Two years ago I sat on the jury—I have been writing pieces for *Città* on industrial projects, so in Italy I am a critic. Of course, that isn't really why I was picked. The editor-in-chief wanted to make a friendly gesture. Then it turned out that we didn't give Charlie's piece of dreck in Hamburg a prize, not even an honorable mention. Of course, later he got the Schnitzler Prize for it, which is what he really wanted, but in the meantime he made a huge fuss, wrote a five-page protest to the editors—we published highlights from it and our reply—and he even got the deans at Columbia and Yale to issue statements about how the whole thing was an anti-American outrage and so on. He sent a letter to me too saying I was personally to blame because I pull all the strings, so I wrote back saying I don't answer crank mail! Since then he is polite when we meet, in this elaborate manner he has developed to go with being a great maestro, and behind my back he says the nonsense that gets repeated to me. When he arrived here, he told Edna that I have been seen picking up male prostitutes in Rome!

Have you?

I was titillated by the turn the conversation had taken, but not totally surprised. He was single, and yet, in the three years I had known him, I had never met a woman he was connected with or seemed to be pursuing. In Kate's opinion, that showed he was a capon, interested only in money and gossip. I tended to accept the proposition, first put to me by my gym teacher at prep school, that there are no sexless lives. As Arthur was rich and extroverted, I found it difficult to believe that masturbation was his principal outlet. Therefore, I had constructed three theories to explain my friend's lack of a known female companion: he was faithful to a married mistress, probably living in Geneva where he officially resided and spent a good deal of time; he disliked wasting time on courtships and resorted to call girls and similar sordid solutions; or he was a very quiet fairy. I knew that there was no lack of those at Harvard, some so discreet that their secret was only known through the compulsive indiscretions of their best friends; why shouldn't they flourish in international business?

Arthur raised his eyebrows. Unfortunately for Charlie, no! I think Charlie has put me at the head of the plot against him because, although he and I have known each other for years—socially—we have never given him any business. Why should we? He is too expensive. There are good architects in Europe, with good names, who work for one-half of what he asks and manage to finish their buildings on time. What we couldn't tell him under *Città* rules is that the jury never even considered his building because the editors didn't propose it! And that is because the editor-in-chief, a very artistic queen, thinks Charlie isn't very nice.

Here he made a disparaging gesture, intended to signify a limp wrist.

I'll see you at dinner, he concluded. You should ask Edna to put you next to Laura. Be nice to her. *C'est une affaire*— still young, organs in good working order, chic apartment in Milan, house in the country, and the *poverina* is all alone.

I had no previous experience with Jews like Arthur. Clearly, he was invited by people—indeed was on terms of complete intimacy with them—who didn't ordinarily have Jewish friends. He just as readily told jokes about Jews that would have been considered unacceptably offensive by Jews I knew on the Law School faculty and Borscht Circuit jokes

in which the goy is an idiot. It seemed to me that, in an
aloof way, he usually ended up calling a spade a spade, an
expression I was learning not to use. I decided to do as he
suggested.

MORE PEOPLE than had turned out the evening before
were gathered in the dining room, where chiaroscuro vil-
lagers, holding each other by the hand or the arm, circled
Pulcinella and flashed longing grins at the guests. Instead of
the long table there were round tables for six on the terrace.
I found my place card; although I had said nothing to Edna, it
was between Laura's and Toby's. So this evening he would
be at dinner. Rodney was next to the boy, then Charlie and a
California woman with false eyelashes and jewelry in the
shape of giant teeth. On the other side of Laura was the director of the Rockefeller establishment. He seemed to be on
a mission to the California woman; I saw him preaching at
her even before we sat down. The lecture, about social trend
indicators and their use in the study of Chicano elites, continued while we ate the pasta. I introduced Toby to Laura
and told her that he had been teaching me backgammon
while everyone else was absorbing culture. She enveloped
me in a smile directed at Toby and began to question him
about school, the work he was doing at Charlie's office, and
his plans for university studies. It turned out she had a niece
his age in Florence who intended to go to college in the
States. She offered to have them meet. He said yes at once,
eagerly, with the easy grace I had earlier liked so much, ex-
plaining he was worried about the academic level of his
boarding school in anything other than mathematics, not

good at all in English composition or in history, while he hoped to become a journalist. Perhaps he couldn't get into any university and should find a job on a paper through his father, the way his father had got him a job with Charlie. Laura was given to alternating abruptly between English and Italian; the admirable child followed her lead, speaking as distinctly and, I thought, as elegantly as she. I began to think that a candidate like him, out of left field, might in due time be helped to gain admission to Harvard—if I made sure the right person, capable of seeing past the standing of the Swiss school and even Toby's standard examination scores, should they turn out to be spotty, studied his case. Illogically, my benevolent intentions gained strength as I observed Laura. She had turned in the boy's direction and was leaning forward; her arm rested against my sleeve, it was naked, and she made no move to take it away. I decided that the red of her jersey dress went perfectly with her hair; earlier, I would have thought the combination was impossible. The light at the center of the table was strong; it turned Laura's suntan into an ashen pallor. She was probably a little older than I had first supposed. What did Arthur mean about her organs, and how had that information come to him? It occurred to me that I might experimentally touch her knee with mine; she returned the pressure, and I perceived a smile directed at the boy that could have been intended for me.

A platter of lake fish followed the ravioli. Rodney warned us about the bones. They were treacherous; Edna wouldn't have allowed the fish to be served if the oil lamps they had found the previous winter in Portugal did not give such a bright light. Even the California woman fell silent as we concentrated on removing them. Laura finished first and began to explain to me the proper technique for deboning fresh-water *frittura*; her entire leg was pressed against mine. I chimed in, stupidly, about bones in fillets of shad.

I had noticed that Charlie, even as he spoke with Rodney, had been listening to the conversation between Toby and Laura. Now he addressed Rodney with a deliberate emphasis, which left no doubt that his remarks were to be heard by the entire table.

It is a risky business when a man such as I, responsible, accustomed to caution and old forms of courtesy, undertakes—be it for the brief space of a summer—to nurture and guide the young son of a friend. Distant friend, to be sure, not one of those links forged when we were malleable and so innocently receptive, like my friendship with Max. What a joy to be reunited with you through the intercession of our hosts!

He put his left hand to his eyes, as though to stop a tear, and ceremoniously raised his wineglass to me and then to Rodney.

One has not seen the youth, if indeed in one's distracted contemplation of the surroundings one deigned to notice him, the resonant voice continued, since he was a child—since a lunch, or perhaps tea, in the garden of his father's house in the hills above Beirut. Sweet smell of jasmine! His gracious mother—such a tragedy!—would have been there. To her alone this fortunate child owes his complexion. Look at him, he is blushing! Lips like rubies swimming in a sea of milk. Of course, the Levantine bandit's eyes, the fierce nostrils, the pride—that is his father. A great man, and dangerous like all great men.

Here Charlie reached past Rodney, grasped Toby's chin, and rotated his face first toward Laura and me, and then toward the California woman, so that we could all see for ourselves, until Toby, tossing his head like a rebellious colt, managed to free himself. I observed with astonishment not only these proceedings but also Charlie's fingers. These being on his right hand, they were almost brown from nicotine, and they ended in uncared-for, long cracked nails. Earlier, Charlie had mopped his plate clean of the pasta sauce with a little piece of bread. I would not have liked to have these fingers on my face.

I have made him angry! That too is a risk—the affection of an older comrade misunderstood, taken for unbecoming familiarity. Forgive me, Toby. The risk I had in mind was much more grave: that of an unworthy choice. Time and attention wasted, like seed the villein scatters on rocky soil. Fair is as fair does! Lilies that fester smell far worse than weeds! Luckily you are like the mysterious youth: unmoved, cold, and to temptation slow. May it ever be thus! For you have talent—promise that I will turn into fulfillment and plenitude. That is, my dear Toby, why I beg you not to speak of newsrooms and copyboys or meetings with Florentine adolescents—though surely Laura's niece, like her beautiful aunt, is most distinguished. A high calling awaits you: be a builder, maker, artist! Live in solitude! My studio will be your Harvard and your Yale!

Charlie paused and raised his glass again, this time to

Toby. There was no reason to think the tirade would not continue after he had drained it. A vast blush covered Toby's cheeks.

The California woman tittered. That sure will save a lot of tuition. Mr. Swan, you are too much!

Or the rest of us are too little, obliged the Rockefeller villa director. Apprenticeship is a noble tradition, the key to creating elites, especially the one we have been discussing. If only the custom could be revived!

IN LAURA'S BED that night, lying on my back, careful not to move lest I wake her—she was gripping me with her hand—myself at first quite unable to find sleep in that position, I chuckled at the liberating effect Arthur's choice of words had had on me. They were no accident. He had my number. Later, already in that state where thought drifts into dream, I listened to the furious, whistling noise outside the window, which I recognized as a gale that must have risen suddenly, and marveled at the day's other encounters and the change in Charlie. At college, like many former boarding-school heroes, he had the sort of assurance that is conferred by success on the river and with the faster debutantes, and a pomposity about the worldly and cultural advantages he had derived from weekends in New York and long vacations in Europe. Since then he had become a busy, powerful celebrity. But these declamatory passions, the insistent familiarity? Was he taking drugs? I was curious how much time would pass before I saw him again. My sleep was interrupted by Laura. She was shaking me by the shoulder and asking whether I could hear the screams. After a moment, over the wind and the desperate clapping of some open shutter, I distinguished a man's voice, howling as though life were leaving his lungs together with the air. I said to Laura, Let's go to the window. We spoke in whispers, although the villa's walls were thick and the noise outside unbearable.

We could see crisscrossing beams of light at the edge of the water. That was where the screams were coming from. I told Laura I would go to look, and quickly put on my clothes. Outside the house, the force of the wind astonished me. It was blowing down the lake from the Alps, in brutal, cold spasms. I ran toward the lights. Rodney was there, and Arthur and Edna and some Italian men who looked as though they worked on the place. It was they and Rodney who held the flashlights, training them on the area between the steps leading from the terrace to the water, where the big launch was moored. On those steps, majestic, his pajamas gleaming like a marble arch, was Charlie, his bare feet on the moss-covered stone, his back taut, his arms pushing against the hull of the launch. The man whose screams I had heard was still in the water, eyes shut, grasping Charlie's feet. Charlie was giving directions, and Rodney and one of the workmen took up positions on both sides of him. While he strained, they slowly lifted the man and then carried him to the terrace. There they laid him on a blanket and covered him with another. The screams stopped. He was only whimpering and twitching. Somebody said the ambulance was certainly taking its time. I asked Arthur what had happened. He explained that Charlie had heard the screams and ran to the lake, on his way waking up Rodney, who got the others. Apparently the boatman—that was the man pulled from the water—had gone to the lake to see how the launch and the other boats were doing in the wind. He must have seen that the launch had dragged its mooring and was going to smash unprotected against the steps. Perhaps he tried to fend it off. That was probably when the accident happened. Whether he slipped on the moss or from the deck was unknown, but as we could see he found himself in the water, crushed between the boat and the stone each time the boat lurched. Charlie was there first and managed to hold the boat away until the man was lifted out, something no one else would have had the strength to accomplish.

As we spoke, Charlie and Rodney finished various complicated arrangements concerning rubber tires, fenders, and the other boats. Charlie noticed me and waved jovially as he put on a robe of black and yellow brocade. It seemed that he had left it on the balustrade before undertaking to separate the elements. Taking a flask from the pocket, he drank a swig and passed it to me.

Here, he said, it's good whiskey. Now I hear the police and the ambulance. Too bad. They'll get him to a hospital. If the son of a bitch lives, he will be a cripple. He would be better off dead.

II

THE RITZ in Boston. A bank in King of Prussia. In the sitting room of a suite above the Public Garden, an old woman stares straight ahead, at nothing. Bony feet in newly shined black pumps crossed on a stool. Its petit point matches the wing chair. White nylon stockings. Calves crooked as though from a lifetime of hugging the saddle. It's the monstrous weight of her body. The flab begins above the knees: there are rolls upon rolls of it under the gray flannel dress, and it has invaded her neck and cheeks. Only feet and hands have been spared. Three strands of pearls. Pale pink hair set in neat curls. Her lips are cracked, although when she leaves the hotel it is always in a closed car. She dabs at them with a stick of grease. My cousin, Emma Hafter Storrow. Thirty years earlier, after the end of the war, already long widowed, she closed the house on Commonwealth Avenue, her father-in-law's astounding wedding gift, forever useless. Her sons had fallen, neither the lilies nor the tuberoses from the glass conservatory would frame a nuptial altar in the rich church in Copley Square. Along the Charles, cars speed on the drive built with Storrow money. That money too unneeded. In sprawling

King of Prussia, from businesses that deface the landscape of her childhood, a nameless river of cash flows to the bank her own father, Judge Maximilian Hafter, founded. The shares are in her trust; she knows how rich she is to the last dime.

No Storrows left; except for her, no Hafters. Because she is the last descendant of the judge's father, after her death she may send the money where she wishes. By appointment. The Hafters were abolitionists. If she does nothing, a Negro orphanage in Alabama will inherit. That's written into the trust. She tells me about the bank lawyer, who visits every quarter. Her cataracts have thickened. She requires that the figures be read aloud. Each time he mentions the "power" and the document she must sign if she would exercise it, she chortles. What has he against those damn pickaninnies?

When I knock, the door opens at once. I enter. The companion, really a nurse, Mrs. Leahy, shows me in and withdraws. Her room is beyond Mrs. Storrow's bedroom. I always knock on Mrs. Leahy's door first. This is our custom; Cousin Emma has never liked to rise from her chair. She chuckles over my name: Maximilian Hafter Strong. The great-grandson of her father's uncle, named after her father, the judge. Why? Did my parents, the professor of agriculture at a Rhode Island state college and his librarian spouse, think it droll to bestow such a large name on a tiny baby, did they like its exotic ring, like some explorer of the Amazon? Her own Maximilian and Hugh were alive when this Max was born; the Christmas cards regularly received and acknowledged so long as the librarian lived were the only commerce between them. None other was offered or sought. In the end, it was she who summoned me into her presence. Out of boredom. How many times since then has she told me the story, how many times has she turned the matter over in her mind?

Although it lacks of noon, I mix gin-and-tonics in purple Venetian tumblers. She likes them half-gin and half-Schweppes. Never mind the hour, she says, here the sun is always over the yardarm. The silver, glass, and china are hers, brought from Commonwealth Avenue, together with the Queen Anne and Chippendale pieces, silk rugs, and flower paintings. The hospital bed Mrs. Leahy cranks up and down is the only alien object. That is a recent acquisition; it marks Cousin Emma's last visit to Phillips House. That's the field of her battles with cancer: both breasts lost and it's not over.

The chocolate mints are in the blue Canton dish beside her. She eats them quickly and offers me the last one. Take it, I am not dead yet. I can send Leahy to buy more.

I laugh. From the sideboard I take a package I think I have managed to conceal until then. Lindt miniatures, dark chocolate, bittersweet. Cousin Emma's favorite, purchased at Cardullo's in Harvard Square. She points to her cheek and waits for my kiss. Another round of drinks, it's Sunday, the time to indulge. I cheat artfully, only pretending to pour gin in mine. This too is one of our customs. How else will I manage to do the work I have set aside for the afternoon?

Lunch. Mock turtle soup, turkey hash, and baked apples. Mrs. Leahy fetches the splits of champagne from the closet fridge, and also pills on a little silver dish. Mrs. Storrow drinks Veuve Clicquot when it's not time for cocktails. Corks reverentially twisted by the waiter leave the bottles with a mere sigh. He serves the food and waits on a chair in the corridor until she rings. Except when asked, Mrs. Leahy takes meals in her own bedroom; it makes Mrs. Storrow nervous to watch her eat, she is so slow; besides, she doesn't like having that Irish woman at the table. She points out that I eat fast, like a Hafter. More champagne. Leahy must fetch it, she won't have me rummaging in the bedroom. Past the cloud of the cataracts she squints at me. Thoughts and questions are left unspoken. They crowd her room like souls of the dead. Does she like this distant relative? Blond with brown eyes, that's the Hafter in him, but thin; the resemblance stops with the coloring. Longing for her own sons rises like nausea. She listens to me talk about the summer's vacation in Italy. Como. Belluno. Udine. Expatriate Americans. She will not say: Why are you alive, why were they not born later, like you, a young man who hasn't been to any war?

Mr. Storrow and she took a villa on the Lago di Garda every summer until he died, she informs me; quite unusual, as Mr. Storrow was most fond of ocean sailing. The boys spoke Italian, like little natives! Later, there were too many memories — and those people in black shirts!

I wonder whether other rich ladies noticed that all might not be well in Italy or Germany. I don't put the question. I talk about Laura's house and vineyards and the cooperative that makes white wine with the grapes she grows. Also about her gallery, which I haven't seen.

Cousin Emma wishes to know whether I have made a romantic declaration. That is the expression she used, year after year, about Kate, whom she never met. I think about Laura's organs and shake my head. When I take my leave, she reaches into her corsage and hands me a check. She has given me money before, sometimes at Christmas and on my birthday, but never such a large amount. I try to kiss her again, but she waves me away. She has a strange way of laughing, like a bass giggle. It had to be a big check, she tells me, to fill the space left by her missing bosoms!

Perhaps it is then that the plan takes form: This boy will not have children, he will never marry, or if he marries it will be an old woman. Can I appoint my money and have it stay in the trust? First to this Max, since there is nobody else, and then, if I am right and there are no little Hafter children, to the pickaninnies?

I learned later that the next day she telephoned the bank lawyer.

III

STILL A HERO in China: at the banquet at Quan Ju De, the best of duck restaurants, a two-story duck hospice really, after we had eaten our way through all the recognizable parts of our web-footed friend, and were about to attack bowls of fragrant duck soup that only looked as though it had been made with cream, my friend and mentor, Mr. Dou Lizhen, the chief of the legal department of the Ministry of Foreign Affairs, started his formal toast. I had grown accustomed to these obligatory spurts of oratory, predictable like a bad sonnet, and in fact had already become able to work within the form myself, free of embarrassment or stage fright. Although his English was close to perfect, he spoke in Chinese, for the benefit of our fellow guests. I was the only foreigner. After every couple of sentences he would pause to allow Miss Wang, the young woman who had been assigned to be my guide and guardian, to interpret. I tried to catch the four-tonal directions of a Mandarin speaker's speech, which give distinct meaning to what would otherwise be homonyms, missed most of them, and then, smiling with appropriate modesty, relaxed as the beautiful Miss Wang, standing at parade-ground attention beside Mr. Dou, rattled on, in her brisk BBC manner, about the bridges of friendship I had built through my work on the joint venture law, the many times my Chinese friends and I would walk over these bridges hand in hand (here I wanted to shout, Wang and Dou, block that metaphor!) straight into the open doors of the new China, and how, in the spirit of mutual benefit and with due regard to the four great principles of modernization decreed by the newly minted Chairman Deng, my seminar on contract law problems had strengthened the relations between our countries. Normally, when the speaker had treated these main themes, he stopped—unless by way of a coda there was to be an anecdote about me, and I rather thought that this time a personal touch might be in order. Instead, my state of devil-may-care ease induced by glass after glass of mao-tai gave way to watchfulness as I heard my Mr. Dou recommend that President Reagan, having recovered from Hinckley's bullets (Dou put that more periphrastically), give full respect to America's great leader Mr. Nixon and study deeply his ways of bringing peace to the world. I knew that minutes after he sat down I would have to be on my feet and in my answer touch on that very subject, as to which it would not do to disagree with the previous speaker. Fortunately, he did not go into the matter deeply. That made it possible—after the quiz-kid feat of addressing each of my fellow duck eaters by his full name as I went around the table clinking glasses—to speak with tranquil conviction of the strength of the personal ties that bound us, my taste for Peking duck in all of its manifestations, and the resolution I had formed to return to China whenever the "relevant authorities" found it convenient—and then to end on an elegant and noncommittal note. I drank to the Shanghai Communiqué, the ninth anniversary of which had just passed. A puff of added inspiration, and I raised my glass also to Harvard University. After all, was it not Harvard that had loosed Henry Kissinger, Nixon's improbable Sancho Panza, upon America, China, Vietnam, Cambodia, and so many other interesting locations on our tired planet?

By the time the banquet was over, the only diners left in the downstairs part of the restaurant were our drivers, lingering over the remains of a chauffeurs' meal. The private dining room we had occupied was windowless; we had not seen the sky grow dark over Beijing. Now we stood on the sidewalk, beside the huddle of black cars, shaking hands in that city's vast and obscure silence broken only by low-pitched human voices and the dring-dring of an occasional bicycle bell. The yellow rectangles of light framed by the restaurant's windows and its door filled one with confused longing. Miss Wang and an older bureaucrat of uncertain rank installed me in the car assigned for my use and then got in themselves to accompany me to the hotel. I had come to understand the practicality of that polite gesture, which was repeated by dinner companions every evening: afterward, the driver would deposit them wherever they lived, probably miles away, at the edge of Beijing's endless outskirts.

The next day was Saturday; work ended at noon, or possibly—I had not penetrated that particular mystery—at the start of the sacrosanct rest period that precedes the lunch hour. But I had realized early on that it was useless and possibly annoying to my clientele of civil servants to try to conduct my seminar on Saturday mornings. As a result, I enjoyed Western-style weekends, devoted to sleeping late, as a compensation for the absurdly early morning hour when, according to local custom, I started operations on the days I taught, and to long visits to the Forbidden City. I felt happiest there; my predilection amused my hosts. Reluctantly but wisely, they gave up organizing visits to ball-bearing factories, model schools, and establishments in which I might have observed the industrial confection of Tang-dynasty horses or folk art objects. There was a difference, however, between respecting my choice and allowing me to be unsupervised. Miss Wang accompanied me to the Imperial Palace and on the walks I liked to take at the end of the afternoon in the Muslim quarter south of Tiananmen Square. If I wanted to play hooky and be alone with my thoughts I pleaded the urgent necessity of preparing my course, implying that I would stay in the hotel. Then, feeling guilty, jaunty, and sly, I would stride westward on Chang An Boulevard, the blue-clad crowd, itself in constant motion, parting before me magically like the Red Sea.

I called her Miss Wang in public, and also in my thoughts. When we were alone, I used her first name, Jun Jun, because she considered that more friendly. And I was far from disliking her presence, notwithstanding my occasional rebellious search for solitude. The Mao suit was still de rigueur in China, for men and women, as was the absence of all makeup. The garment worn over it was almost universally a lined green field jacket or an army coat without military insignia. Miss Wang, though, was the owner of a wine-colored ski parka, purchased in Canada, where she had visited with a trade mission. She wore this high-fashion object with pride, notwithstanding the recent mild weather, and what with its bulk and the floating nature of those blue suits, the notion I had of her body owed more to inflamed speculation than to anything I had actually observed. I imagined her wonderfully thin, but not bony, with only dark aureoles where her breasts should be, and no hips at all. Her legs, I hoped, would be shapely, worthy of the pretty, black-slippered feet on which she trotted beside me. Quite short—her head arrived just above my elbow—she had the unspoiled face of a child caught midway between a smile and a pout. At times, when I wanted her to look at some gargoyle on a palace roof, I could not resist tugging on her pigtails. I thought at first it was imprudent of the ministry to give me an interpreter-guide such as she, and wondered whether it was not, in fact, a conscious experimental provocation, undertaken with the thought that if I succumbed to her charms the incident could be stored away for some possible future use. Gradually, I came to the conclusion it was absurd to suspect it could be in anyone's interest to embarrass me while I was performing services China urgently wanted. In any case, I was determined to remain on the ground of good comradeship with Miss Wang, saving the intimacies I urgently desired and imagined for solitary meditation in my hotel room, and the time when her dream of coming to study law in America might be miraculously realized.

We parted in the drive of the Beijing Hotel. She said she would come back in the morning for our usual palace visit. This time, I did not object.

Thanks to Mr. Dou's fortuitous family tie with the manager of the hotel, I was living in the fortress-like central building, constructed long before World War II, and not in one of the dreadful additions, the earlier of which was built with Russian assistance and on a Soviet model, and the later, even more tawdry, by Canadian interests. Accordingly, I had a room of bourgeois proportions and a bathroom equipped with large, old-fashioned fixtures. Many of the other rooms and suites in this part of the hotel were used as representative offices of Swiss and German banks and well-known industrial corporations; on my own floor were located the combination sleeping quarters and offices of several American law firms waiting for clients to sprout from the soil of new capitalism. But, as an initial matter, my presence in the Beijing Hotel—instead of the squalid Friendship establishment, where I might have been together with other visiting professors, Eastern European engineers, and Japanese businessmen—was due to the change in my personal circumstances, which had enabled me to say to the foreign ministry that I needed no stipend and would, moreover, pay all my travel and living expenses if only I was given a car and driver and the opportunity to rent a decent place to stay. My cousin Emma had died the previous year, carried away by a stroke and not, as she had feared, by cancer. Against all reasonable expectations, without ever having uttered a word about it— the thought that I might inherit from her more than a few thousand dollars or a piece of Hafter furniture had never entered my mind—she left me the use of her very large fortune. From a how-to-make-ends-meet law professor I was magically transformed into a man who was potentially rich. Potentially, because the charity that would have received this ton of money had my cousin not chosen to surprise it and me decided to contest the validity of her bequest. I was convinced that the challenge was frivolous, an opinion shared by the trustees, who, without awaiting the outcome of the litigation, had begun to pay me an allowance that lifted me many stories above my old existence.

THE NEXT MORNING, in one of the deserted eastern courtyards of the Forbidden City—where grass advancing timidly across the glazed tile roofs of detached palaces bears witness to decades of neglect—I was in fact discussing with Miss Wang, quite seriously this time, what needed to be done to get her into a Law School program at Harvard. Paradoxically, it was best to apply for a year of graduate work, on the basis of not much more than her good intentions and the undeniable fact that no one in her generation had received a conventional education. The Cultural Revolution had taken care of that. Then if she did well—her intelligence and grasp of the English language were so fine that I felt confident she would—one could hope she would be admitted to the regular program of studies and, in due course, would emerge as an American lawyer. She needed to get permission to leave China, and a certain amount of specific backing from her ministry as well, since the Law School's center for Far Eastern studies made no bones about wanting to be on good terms with the Chinese authorities. One would have to be able to show that she was a horse that would run on the track of Chinese bureaucracy when the time came for her to go back home. The question of funds we could face later. I told her I thought that problem could be solved: there were regular Law School scholarships and possibilities of foundation support as well. A strong recommendation from me would do no harm, and she could count on it. Because I thought the departure for America had to be her project, I took care not to let her guess that, in a pinch, I might cover the tuition myself.

The powerful, melodious beauty of the place we were in, forms and colors recombined in seemingly unending variations, and its mad and tragic history always awakened in me a sort of heightened sympathy: it was as though I were on the verge of crying tears of gratitude. Exactly what for, I don't know. Perhaps it was quite simply the good luck of being in that place; possibly, in a circular fashion, I was moved by my own ability to feel so deeply. In any event, I responded strongly to the blush of happiness that appeared on Miss Wang's face: she also liked this Imperial Palace and its memories—in fact, of all the Chinese with whom I had walked there, she knew the most about its customs and history and was freest of the errors abounding in simplified guidebooks and stupidly repeated by official guides. At this moment, though, she had been transported to the land for which her years at the foreign language institute had been an unintended preparation. There she would at last use every phrase of those dialogues among lively, optimistic students she had memorized so well out of her schoolbooks. She had glimpsed the magnificence of it for such a brief moment only, with her group of comically dressed trade officials, deadly serious behind gold-toothed grins, when she made that single trip to Ottawa and Toronto. She embraced me, and I was about to kiss her on both cheeks, where they were reddest, when from behind I heard a voice I could not fail to recognize. It was Charlie Swan's.

The colors are imperial, my love, he was saying, only the son of heaven had the right to these yellows, greens, and blues, and the potent red. That is why the rest of Beijing is gray: it wears a smock of humility, like the puritan maidens who were my great-aunts and cousins. At the ends of the cornices, dragons and sea monsters, to frighten away evil spirits. You have seen these same protectors displayed in bas-relief on the sloping marble slabs that lead from the court-yards to each palace the emperor might enter, like this one here. His sedan chair would pass over the zone thus purified, the bearers on each side mounting the steps that are parallel to it.

I considered prolonging the embrace of Miss Wang, and keeping my face buried in the shoulder of her parka, until he had moved past us, but curiosity got the better of me. I looked in his direction. Even heavier and larger than in Italy, where I had last seen him, and in deference to the season wearing a tweed suit of such exquisite heather tones that I wondered whether it had been woven for him alone by old crones on the Isle of Wight, he was otherwise unchanged. He held the arm of a beautiful and blond young man. It was Toby, the playful Eros of the Rumorosa.

Max, you wicked snoop, boomed the voice thus distracted from architectural history, which one of my incantations has summoned you here, with such mischievously delayed ef-fect? All my invitations declined, offers to visit ignored, and yet here you are, in the one place where I would have thought Toby and I could be tête-à-tête! Or is it tit for tat, since we find you in a pleasantly delicate situation with this young lady?

He laughed generously at his own joke.

Genuine pedagogic pleasure, Charlie, nothing more. I was congratulating Miss Wang on the road map we have just worked out for her future legal studies! She is a student in the seminar I am leading, the best interpreter in China, and my true friend.

I did not think that Charlie measured the consequences of joking, even in this empty corner of the Imperial Palace, about a "delicate situation" between this poor child and a guest of the Chinese government's to whom she had been assigned as a guide; the disparity between the risk to her and my achieving an unexpectedly clearer understanding of the nature of his feelings for Toby was enormous. I now think that my habitual caution led me to exaggerate, but at the time I truly believed that nothing in China concerning foreign "friends" went unobserved. I resolved to remind Charlie not to joke about Miss Wang and me if we met again, and not to mention the incident, even if he kept back her name, in anecdotes with which he might wish to titillate his Chinese contacts.

The object of my worry seemed unconcerned by the conversation and, in fact, glad to meet these two men, one of whom was near to her in age. Glancing at me as though to see whether I would object, she proposed that we continue the visit together.

Splendid! decreed Charlie, let's go to the eunuchs' quarters. They are a great curiosity. Toby will be amused.

I interjected mildly that they were, on a diagonal, at the opposite end of the Forbidden City, and that by the time we had gotten there, looked around, and returned to the East Gate, where Miss Wang had told the driver to meet us, the poor man would be in a state of anxiety and the hotel kitchen closed. I could think of no other place we might have lunch. Charlie brushed these worries aside, saying that his car was waiting at Coal Hill, only a few minutes from where he proposed to go. We would then have plenty of time, both to rescue my driver and to have lunch. It turned out that he and Toby were also at the Beijing Hotel. And so we set off, passing the great ceremonial reception halls and the very small palace where the emperors actually lived, and then turned toward the quarters of the empress, the concubines, and the eunuchs. Charlie was well informed about the palace and had the sort of eye one would expect in an architect for tricks of perspective, vistas that suddenly appeared in the moonlike opening in a wall, and the effects of occasional asymmetry in these marvelously repetitious groupings of buildings and open spaces. He resumed with brio the lecture to Toby the encounter with us had interrupted—the chance to address a larger audience may have acted as a stimulus—sometimes pulling on the boy's sleeve when he thought his attention flagged or taking hold of his ear to make sure his head was turned in the direction of the medallion or other detail of decoration he wanted him to notice.

We reached the melancholy dwelling place of the eunuchs: a square space of marble, formed by four low buildings containing cells with vaulted ceilings. Their doors opened on the courtyard. Standing at the balustrade of the adjacent terrace, one looked down on the dull roofs. The place could have served as a stable. Ghostly presences—this was where memories of a lost world seemed to me most present, almost physically, as though some acrid scent had lingered undisturbed in the still air.

Society was turned upside down here, announced Charlie. The perversity of its structure will entertain and instruct you. No comradeship of men. The emperor alone with his sons and women lived in the Imperial Palace, and the sons only while they were small children. Afterward, they were moved out, away from the Forbidden City, until the son who had been selected to succeed returned to ascend the Peacock Throne. It was the fear of assassination: where two males meet, one will try to kill the other. For that same reason, the choice of the heir remained occult; should it become known, his envious brothers or their mothers might assassinate him. So within the walls of this enclave no one but the emperors' women—wives, concubines, women servants, and, of course, eunuchs. Men who had stopped being men. The women the emperor fucked each had her name inscribed on an ivory marker. Like your backgammon pieces! In the evening, an important eunuch presented all the markers to the emperor and he chose one. Then the eunuchs went to the woman's house, stripped her so that she had no place to conceal a knife or a vial of poison, and brought her, wrapped in a blanket, to the imperial bed.

Why only one a night, Miss Wang? he asked abruptly. Why not many? After all, it's said that they hardly ever came, you know, ejaculated, just wanted to bathe the member as much as possible in a woman's juices. Absorb them through the rigid phallus. Juices bringing health and longevity, like vitamins! Do you know the answer? I may be wrong: perhaps every night they brought one woman after another!

I am so very sorry, it isn't mentioned in the guidebooks I have studied.

Having delivered this standard reply of a well-trained guide to most questions about Chinese history before liberation, Miss Wang giggled very hard.

How curious what guidebooks will omit, Miss Wang. And what is the present position with regard to women's juices? Do you know that?

Now Toby was giggling as well, besides having turned beet red, while I wondered whether each time I met Charlie it would be necessary to think of braining him.

I needn't have bothered. Miss Wang could take care of herself. It can't matter, Mr. Swan, she replied, family planning is obligatory in China, as you probably know, and it requires Chinese men to use contraceptive devices.

Quite right, I should have thought of that myself. And a good reason for substituting the pill! But we must get on with our eunuchs. These were volunteers, Toby, often married and fathers of families! I don't know that there was a competitive examination, as with other offices in China. Men who applied for the position, and were lucky enough to be accepted, sat down on a stool rather like a *chaise percée*, and someone underneath went snip. The testicles were placed on a shelf, in an individual jar marked with the owner's name. That way the eunuchs could be buried with their balls and be complete again, a matter of crucial importance for the Chinese, right Miss Wang?

Charlie had not noticed that he had lost the indigenous part of his public. Miss Wang had apparently decided to walk ahead of us. He raised his eyebrows in what could have been a sign of disappointment and continued.

The superstition led to a comical scene when the last emperor fled and this establishment was shut down. The old eunuchs all departed, a suitcase full of spare pajamas in one hand and the jar containing the balls in the other. What a ball!

Balls, said Toby, why is this stuff supposed to entertain or instruct me? It's disgusting from beginning to end.

That's the point, baby, that's the point. A woman is a hole filled with juice that starts to smell like fish upon contact with air. Happiness, comradeship, cannot be built upon the cult of the hole.

Here Charlie threw his arms wide open and shouted to the empty space:

But to the girdle do the gods inherit,
Beneath is all the fiends': there's hell, there's darkness,
There is the sulphurous pit, burning, scalding,
Stench, consumption. Fie, fie, fie! Pah, pah!

And looking around him with great satisfaction, because his memory had served him well, he repeated: Fie, fie, fie! Pah, pah!

Afterward we had lunch, all four of us, in the restaurant in my part of the hotel, which was really quite decent and available to clients paying cash and to state guests whose sponsoring organizations had taken a deep breath and decided to register them there, notwithstanding the higher price, rather than in the greasy spoon at the Canadian-built annex. I had been so registered; moreover, on the advice of Miss Wang, at the very beginning of my stay I presented to the maître d'hôtel, who was a young woman probably from the north of China, she was so tall, a silk scarf printed with some flowers. This simple gesture had lifted me to a pedestal of importance I had never enjoyed either at Cronin's or the Faculty Club, the eateries with which the Beijing Hotel restaurant was now tied for first place in my affections. The quality of the welcome I received, and the news I sprang on Charlie that I lived in the old building—he admitted sourly that he and Toby had checked into the Russian horror, a place of cockroaches and thirty-watt lightbulbs—left Charlie temporarily with nothing specific to patronize me about. I relished the moment. The food came in a rush of dishes slammed on the table; prodded by Charlie, we had ordered too much. Miss Wang would have plunged her chopsticks into the platters like a surgeon who questions a wound, delivering to our plates sea cucumbers, noodles, or whatever else was most slippery without a drop of sauce lost in transit, but Charlie, instinctively the paterfamilias, would have none of it. Under his ministrations the tablecloth soon turned into a gloomy, brown Jackson Pollock, the impasto of drippings richest near his own plate. Again, he was pushing food, particularly rice, with his fingers. I averted my eyes and asked Toby, who had spoken only in monosyllables since we left the Forbidden City, whether he had already graduated from college.

I never went.

And what have you been up to?

I've been working on a design for Charlie's New York
office.

Oh.

The answer chilled me. I thought about it during lunch,
which ended only when the waiters, impatient to close,
gathered in a silent circle around our table, and while Miss
Wang and I strolled from the Dongsi mosque through the al-
leys leading to a maze of hutons that had survived the zeal of
the Liberation, peeking into secret and hostile courtyards
and admiring an occasional sculpted gate or a roof decorated
with dragons, and much later, when I rested in my room.
Charlie and Toby had been unable to come with us on the
walk because there were drawings Charlie needed to review.
He was making a presentation to his clients, colossally rich
overseas Chinese planning to build a luxury hotel on the outskirts of Beijing. They had invited him to China. We were to
have a drink, though, before dinner, Charlie, Toby, and I.

I WAITED FOR THEM downstairs, in that part of the lobby
which doubled as a bar. All foreigners of any note who blew
into town—businessmen, journalists, government officials,
do-gooders like me, and an occasional fancy tourist—passed
through it, as well as a great many members of the Chinese
nomenklatura and the sort of gilded youth that had begun to
be visible in Beijing: children of high officials equipped with
one or two items of apparel not conforming to the proletar-
ian dress code, and sometimes looking downright expensive.
Cowboy boots, belted trench coats, sweaters that might have
just walked out of the Paul Stuart window; they wore them
like identification badges. But the background was made up

of a less interesting fauna. Sprawled out in 1930s armchairs upholstered with green or brown plush, their legs and feet a menace to passersby, with bottles of beer, cans of peanuts, and ashtrays overflowing with cigarette butts on the coffee tables before them, these were the Westerners whose principal occupation was waiting. Men. Overweight, guts spilling over their belts. Engineers and salesmen. They waited for the restaurant to open, the bar to close, for the arrival of the ministry employee who was to meet them there or who might convey them to an appointment outside, for a telephone call from Hong Kong, or the hour when it would be right (according to what rules?) to go upstairs to sleep. In the four months I spent going in and out of that place, I do not think I ever saw one of these recumbent figures open a book. Girlie magazines were forbidden in China. I suppose they did their reading in bed.

Charlie showed up alone.

Il fanciullo is indisposed, he said. Headache; might be the grippe; anyway, he has decided to stay in the room. We must be here another ten days, so let us pray to St. Anthony of Padua that it is only a headache. The embassy fellow who met us at the airport claims that the hospital for foreigners is like a morgue. Friendship Hospital! How I wish something here was openly unfriendly!

I offered to mix a martini for him with my own supply of gin and vermouth. Having already consumed one myself, I felt more "openly unfriendly" than usual. In any case, I was tired of Charlie's setting the direction each time we talked. Therefore, as soon as the concoction I had prepared was cradled in his hand—we were drinking out of water glasses—I let him have it: Don't you think it more likely that he is upset by our meeting here, and the lecture on smegma and eunuchs' testicles? He may prefer not to see me a second time today.

Evidently, this attempt to avoid my customary circumlocutions did not impress Charlie. He stirred the martini with his median finger, drank it, and made another one. Remembering his taste for the stuff, I began to wonder whether I had brought enough gin from my room.

You mean that Toby is embarrassed because you have found us out and, in consequence, is hiding? he asked, an immense smile spreading over his face. What a pity you've been playing hard to get—I don't mean it that way, you ass, oops, these aren't words a queer should use—it's just that if you had come to visit me from time to time I would have shown you something of the world that lies outside Cambridge. On second thought, everything you need to know can also be learned in Cambridge, I mean that which was not imparted to you at the Law School and wherever in Rhode Island it was that your mommy brought you up. All you need is a mentor like me. Toby doesn't give a hoot; in New York, Toby is a hot date! It's you, baby, who are embarrassed. And you know why? It's because you don't know how to act with a queer. Possibly you are even a teensy-weensy bit afraid. After all, at your age you are unmarried, you are an intellectual and a part-time aesthete. The profile of a homo! Suppose someone you know who knows about me or who can spot a queer sees us together—or you with the boy!—what will they think? Naughty, naughty! Or suppose, now that I know that you know, I make a pass. Or even better, the delectable

Toby tries one—have you thought of that? And suppose you like it: What happens then? A big pile of emotional *merde* for the respectable, slightly fey law professor! Explosion! Propelled out of the closet he didn't even know he was in! I am a little bit embarrassed too, but for you, because although I suffer fools I don't suffer them gladly. Let's face it, baby, I like you. No, don't worry, not that way!

Here he laughed, wiped his eyes, moved his armchair closer to mine, gave my knee a prolonged exploratory squeeze, and refilled our glasses.

You leave me speechless and ashamed, not just embarrassed.

Nonsense! Get some peanuts and ask your girlfriend in the restaurant to keep a table for us. We might as well dine together—just you and me.

I did as he said. Charlie's cheeks were sagging; he looked gloomy. The effect of nearly straight gin? I doubt it; his tolerance for alcohol was prodigious. I poured another drink. My gesture must have interrupted a train of thought that had distressed him. As though a switch had been turned, I saw his usual alacrity return. He was taking the measure of the hotel guests in our vicinity, staring at them quite openly, his expression successively contemptuous, quizzical, and droll.

Dreadful, he announced. It is my habit, whenever I find myself in a place like this, to check whether there is anyone in sight worthy of being screwed. Zero! I was wise to bring Toby and, of course, lucky to run into you.

He gave my knee another squeeze.

It seemed stupid, and open to being understood as a form of rejection, to change the subject and talk about the new hotel he was going to build, his other work, or American politics, although the latter subject was very much on my mind and he could have given me fresh information, having left New York only a few days earlier. Instead, I told him that his tirade had left me shaken, but also very curious. After all, I knew so little about his life. We had seen each other only once since he got married, perhaps twice—I wasn't quite sure.

That's true, he replied. I wouldn't be surprised if you wanted to hear about the making of a pervert.

I began to protest that I didn't mean to pry, but he stopped me with a particularly hard squeeze of my knee.

Don't be so shittily humorless. I didn't think you were asking about the sort of details you can look up in Krafft-Ebing next time you are in a library. I am keeping those for my memoirs, which I will write only after I turn celibate. I took your remarks as a perfectly appropriate question: How did you get from the man I knew to the man you have become?

I nodded.

The facts are uncomplicated; on the other hand, my nature, or rather the changes in it, and the work accomplished by time to bring about those changes, very mysterious. I was not a closet faggot during the years when we saw each other in Cambridge, or before that at school, or when I married Diane. Certainly, at St. Mark's there were a few rather sweet incidents that today would be called homoerotic. That's an odiously pompous adjective; try to avoid it as your interest in queers continues to grow! Group jerkoffs, a master who would have kissed my bum and everything near it if he had dared, a couple of characters rather like you having wet dreams about my jockstrap. I took it as a tribute—it went with the job! If you are the captain of the crew and look like me you expect little faggots to want to lick your balls, but there was no one whose balls I had the slightest desire to lick. My dick was in fact getting licked by my first cousin—peace, Max, a girl cousin!—who had been thrown out of Milton and was living with my parents, to give her old man a chance to cool off. When the next chapter opens, I am in Korea, not in the fleshpots of Seoul, but in a foxhole, wetting my pants each time I am ordered to climb out and start running up some hill. I did make one visit to a teahouse in Pusan, just before some shrapnel visited me. The dose I got there was taken care of, together with everything else, in the hospital, which was a great piece of timing; the battalion commander would have had me up on charges. Getting the clap was like damaging army property; it ranked with rust in the barrel of your rifle!

One pleasant stop in Hawaii, and we will move along the highway of sex to Harvard and Janie. In the hospital in Honolulu, they did some specialized work on my back and got it into perfect shape. I was immobile for more than two months, though, and, just like in a war movie, a thoughtful nurse—Gauguin's Tehamana on leave from the Art Institute in Chicago—extended her care to my dickey. She quite spoiled the little fellow.

An odd prelude to homosexuality, I remarked.

As usual, you are most perceptive, but we aren't there yet.

He poured the remaining gin into our glasses, and we made our way into the restaurant. I was eager for Charlie to continue his story, but the waitress reduced the number of dishes Charlie ordered by a third, saying that we would be wasting food, which stirred him into what sounded like the beginning of a lecture on *The Theory of the Leisure Class*. He regained his composure when, at my urging, she agreed to produce a bottle of rice wine. He had not yet tried Shaoxing; at the time, it was available in China only rarely.

Sweet Janie, he continued. What a pleasant memory! Weren't you trying at one point to crawl under her Pringle sweater? No, of course it was Edna's, and then goat-legs got you back on a leash! You are one of the happy few to whom I will have confessed this, but Janie and I only necked. I didn't keep my neck in my pants all the time, though, and we played nice games together in bed; in fact, she continued the good work of my cousin and Miss Gauguin. But I never got to insert it. Sometimes Janie claimed she wanted to remain *intacta*, sometimes she said I was too big, and little by little I stopped pressing the point. Looking back on it, particularly when I consider my time with Diane, I think I must have realized it was a very pleasant, undemanding arrangement. Neither crew training nor martinis interfered with it! I ran into Diane at the Cotillion in New York, just as Janie was about to graduate, and Janie had already met that gangster from Chicago—I suspect he forced his way in on the first date!

He snapped his fingers at the waitress, who didn't like it, but got her nevertheless to bring another bottle of Shaoxing. Nectar, he said, only served warm.

Back to Diane. As you may surmise, the families were pleased. I was too. You will recall that we looked remarkably good together. I was starting my training with Gordon Bunshaft. My heart was set on working for him. With Diane's money added to what I had, we immediately set up in a way that was quite handsome. Her parents were very decent too; throughout the season, every weekend I wasn't on charette we would go out to New Jersey to shoot. But, rather quickly, Diane became a serious nuisance about sex—with reason! Between work and drink, I didn't want it all that much, and when I did get the little man up, it was over, so far as I was concerned, as soon as I got him in. Wham bam thank you ma'am! She was willing enough to crank me up by hand and to do the Janie. But I didn't want it; for her it was just the preparation, and what she was preparing me for wasn't what I liked! I managed to put a stop to these efforts by telling her I had a dreadful trauma about oral sex—and I refused to reveal its origin because I couldn't make up my mind whether I should say that I had been bitten or to make up something really lurid. How could I refuse, though, to visit a sex therapist with her, an old prune of a lady doctor in one of those buildings near the New York Hospital? She was full of constructive suggestions: count from one thousand backward to delay ejaculation, fuck in the morning when you are hard anyway, read dirty books together. I think that this sort of thing is best left unsaid—imagine that bit of prudishness coming from my lips! In brief, sex therapy had a negative effect.

1965! The year of the vaginal orgasm! Junior League Bacchantes rampaging through the parlors of the Colony Club! Diane was very advanced. Her women's group decided that diaphragms are demeaning, because the Frau does all the work: she has to stick the thing up her pussy before she is one hundred percent sure she will need it, she must lie down and spread her legs and take it, and finally, when it's all over, more work. The gadget has to be taken out, powdered, and put away in its little box. The solution was to have me wear a condom. That brought the curtain down on my performance. Soon she got a lawyer, a cute little fellow in a derby hat who made house calls—I am referring to an unfortunate time I hit her—and in record time we were divorced.

Am I boring you? he asked while I paid that part of the bill which was not included in my board. Because now we will come to the interesting part, what Scotty Reston would call the watershed event.

There was nothing one could get to drink in the lobby at that hour. I suggested going up to my room, where I had some cognac. We sat down in the two armchairs. It was a strangely chilly evening. Fatigue or excitement, I found I was shivering. I turned on the electric heater.

My condition hadn't escaped Charlie's attention. Are we afraid to be alone with the satyr? Ah, that's better, nothing like a glass of brandy before an open fire! Ha! Ha!

The watershed turned out to be the Vienna woods. I went to Vienna in June, right after the divorce, to look at the Sparkasse and some other Otto Wagner work.

There were ideas of design passing through my head. I was prescient, or I had simply looked at the photographs very well: whichever it was, this work, once I had actually seen it—stared at it as if in a trance—became the grain of sand around which gradually formed the pearl of my artistic invention. Absolute truth, although expressed bombastically. Do you know my Union Bank building in New York? It rises over Madison Avenue exalted and yet humble; every element in its design is a call to order and an echo; I have conceived it so that the surrounding motley structures all take comfort in its presence.

I said truthfully that I found the bank building exceptionally beautiful.

Well, that was what I did downtown. The Vienna woods was where I went to drink wine with an architecture student who had been recommended to me as a combination assistant and guide. Bronzino portrait of a young man, but dressed in a green corduroy suit and reincarnated as a specialist in sex disorders! The diagnosis that had eluded Diane's New York Hospital guru he made the moment we met. One evening, when all the stars were out and the cuckoo sang in the lilac trees, he began the therapy. I have not swerved from the road he traced.

Is this—I mean your having become a homosexual—generally known?

Having become? I prefer being. It's known among the upper set in Sodom, and if one queer is onto a secret, in the next five minutes the rest of the world is informed. If you mean have I come out of the closet, the answer is no! I would like to lead a mass movement back into the closet; it's so cozy.

And you're all right in sex now, the impotence was just with women?

I have told you to read Krafft-Ebing for details, cutie pie. I don't mind talking about girls; that's good clean locker-room fun. The homo stuff is strictly personal!

He leaned over and massaged my knee, as if I had reminded him that it had been neglected since before dinner.

His glass was empty. Apropos of closets, he inquired, is that where you keep that venerable brandy? You seem to be saving it for a rainy day!

I got up and poured him an enormous shot.

He scratched extensively and continued: I will explain to you the presence of Toby, so that he will be spared your hysterics when you meet again. Rest easy, I didn't seduce him that summer when we met at the Joyce caravanserai. It's not my form. He went back to school in Switzerland, but at the end of the year, he ran away. Disappeared for six months or more! His father had the Interpol and every other kind of police looking for him. Not a trace. Then, one day, out of the blue—that's not a pun—he rang my office in New York. Fortunately, I picked up the telephone myself; my secretary might not have put him through. He said he was at a pay phone in the city—he refused to say where—and that he would come to see me if I had clean clothes put in a hotel room where he could first wash and rest. I had some things delivered to the Waldorf, down the street from me, and the next day I saw him. He was a mess. I have kept him with me ever since. Do you believe in the fatal irony of names?

I am not sure I know what you mean.

How odd! I should have thought its incidence would be painfully familiar to a manikin whose ma and pa had the pretention to call him Maximilian! I am obsessed by it. You see, my parents, God rest their souls, were avid readers of Proust. And yet they called me Charles! Private joke or imprudent respect for family tradition? Because I am in fact Charles III. Both my paternal grandfather and great-grandfather had that name, but that was AP, *avant* Marcel. You see, just like Odette, Toby is a pissing tart, and the little bugger isn't even my type.

HE'S GOT A HEADACHE, but I don't think he's hung over; that almost never happens, said Toby the next morning. He said we should go ahead without him.

Miss Wang had asked if she could take that Sunday off, to do laundry and visit her friend at Beijing University. The latter project involved many miles of pedaling. The Chinese I knew used the word "friend" asexually; there was no indication whether this one was a man or a woman, a question that gnawed at me, as this was not the first such expedition. Her wishing to see a girlfriend, in preference to traipsing around Beijing with me and sharing a couple of meals, I found quite natural. If it was a man, her choice did not merely annoy me; a bizarre failure of logic made me consider it foolish, almost unreasonable. What could an afternoon with some deadly serious, bespectacled law student or teaching assistant offer that could compete with me? Even taking account of the total lack of privacy that prevailed at Beida (that's how the university was commonly referred to), I was able to imagine, of course, a certain activity there other than conversation, one from which I had refrained—I assumed that the decision had been mine exclusively—but didn't the delicious tension between us, the fruit of that denial, offer an adequate reward? It occurred to me that if Miss Wang had told me the previous morning about seeing her friend at Beijing University, I might have been less enthusiastically optimistic about her chances at Harvard.

I suggested to Toby that we return to the Forbidden City by what I called the back way: the lively street parallel to Chang An, north of the hotel. We walked past the bicycle repair shop, the establishment where mechanics hammered on mysterious large motors—was this an attempt at repair or the process of turning them into scrap? Elderly men and women, bent almost in half from rheumatism or a lifetime of bearing loads of merchandise, shuffled along, winter vegetables in bags made of netting on their backs. Some looked out of windows or stood in doorways, puffing on long clay pipes. When we got to the canal, other old men were at their t'ai chi exercises, eyes unseeing, as though they were acting out a dream.

The morning was warm and sunny. In one of the courtyards of the palace, there were stone tables with chairs on both sides at which old men who had surely retired long ago played chess. We sat down to watch a game.

Charlie said he talked to you last evening.

That's right. He explained a lot of things I hadn't understood.

He's a good egg. I am very lucky.

I asked Toby whether he liked chess.

No, I just play backgammon and checkers. But it's fun to look at them play.

Then he asked, Are you very disappointed?

By what? I replied cautiously.

Not the gay stuff, that's just how it is. For guys my age, it's not such a big deal. I mean my not going to college and all that. You're a professor, so you must think I'm kind of going down the tubes. You had that hurt expression when I told you yesterday.

My official role as a pedagogue was not something I thought about much in civilian life, outside Langdell Hall, but suddenly I realized that for this poor child—it would be necessary to accustom myself to the fact that he had turned into a young man—I represented constituted authority: a censor who keeps the gates of education and normal life as an adult.

So I said to him, It was a very unexpected meeting. It took me a while to get used to the two of you showing up here all of a sudden, when in my mind you were still on the shore of Lake Como. Don't pay attention to the effect of surprise. I don't think you're finished: there are many ways outside the university to prepare yourself for life, and you have a good start with your languages and travel. If you use your head and read as much as you can, you will do just fine. You must be learning all sorts of things at Charlie's office and from being with Charlie. Who knows? If you feel the need of it, there will always be time for college or a professional school later.

I was pretty badly screwed up, but it's true, Charlie is teaching me a lot, if I can stick to it.

He gave me a big open smile, which seemed genuine, like when he told me it was all right to paddle along at his side in the swimming pool at the Rumorosa.

IV

RUN SLOWLY, horses of the night! How often would I whisper those words to myself during the first decade of my prosperity? That wish was not granted to me. Instead, events, experiences, time itself accelerated, like grains of sand when the beach is whipped by a storm. Perhaps it was the effect of the contrast with my previous mode of existence. I had been used to living like a superannuated graduate student: in small spaces, taking measured steps. Perhaps it was my age. So little had changed inside me, and yet, in a couple of years, I would, with so much of my past unperceived, really not felt, turn fifty.

Slides of jumbled vacations—uncherished, neglected, almost embarrassing—one has resolved to set in order someday. Let me stand aside and display them. Look at Max as I see him now, such as I was then in the distant whirlwind.

VESPASIAN WAS NUTS to say money has no smell. It's like the mating stuff that skunks spray, except it draws the rich, the not so rich, and the famous of both sexes; gays too. Now that Max is wealthy, they're all over him. Such easy manners: colleagues who have never spoken to him outside of faculty meetings, those Brattle Street and Beacon Hill intellectuals he doesn't know even by sight, invite him for meals and drinks, or to watch sports on television—the latter invitations he never accepts—as though he had always been there, an intimate friend of the household. Max has finally discovered the secret password of the Western world; Arthur and he are still friends, but, in his new circumstances, what is to stop Max from getting into Ali Baba's cave on his own?

Max is respected, possibly liked, at the Law School; that's because he doesn't ask for favors or belong to either of the cliques that wish to transform the place. Teaches conscientiously. His letters to the graduate studies committee and the financial aid office, followed by casual visits to assistant deans who manipulate decisions of this sort, have the desired effect. Miss Wang is admitted, with a full scholarship. The housing office assigns her to a regular dormitory: he insists on it, in preference to a room in one of those communal apartments in Somerville or Waltham; he knows that Chinese graduate students stick together like steamed rice. That would be a waste of the Harvard experience, he tells her. The point is to be with Americans, working through the same problems as they; there is more to a legal education than reading casebooks.

That's also the argument he eventually uses to get her out of his own place. When he sleeps with her, the night of her arrival, it's as though some terrible thirst were at last slaked. He thinks he is filling to the brink the lithe, violent tube that passes for her body. It's also keeping a wordless pact made in the Forbidden City. It seems that neither of them had doubts about its terms.

But he isn't ready for a Chinese concubine, just as he doesn't keep a dog or a cat. It makes him nervous that she washes his shirts and scours the bathroom, although the cleaning woman has just done it, that she likes to sit in his lap. She thinks they should eat at home: the smell of the vegetables she stirs in the frying pan for dinner clings to her skin. There is a way she has of bringing him cups of tea when he works at his desk that makes him unable to concentrate. When he packs her off to the Harkness he gives her a key and tells her she must call before she comes over.

In no time at all, she asks if she may introduce a new friend. He is a Chinese scholar, that's what he calls himself, at the Business School; same model, Max thinks, as the friend he imagined she might have at Beida. They have dinner à trois in the Chinese restaurant on Massachusetts Avenue across the street from Wigglesworth. The scholar insists on paying. Miss Wang continues to sleep with Max, but it's all much lighter now; they have a good time when they talk, like in Beijing; her first examinations are approaching, and he helps her get prepared. One day, he receives a letter from Miss Wang. It covers two large sheets of pink paper with flowers in the upper-right-hand corner. The handwriting is beautiful; there are really no mistakes in her English. She thanks him for her new life and apologizes. The scholar and she are in love. She is returning the key to Sparks Street. It's just as well, considering how much time Camilla is spending there.

SHE HAS BLOND HAIR, green eyes, and long legs. Doesn't use deodorant; or perfume, either. First woman he has known whose armpits aren't shaved. An English girl, living in Cambridge, Massachusetts. Backed by a first-class degree from a women's college at Oxford, she does something or other at the Fogg. It turns out to be conservation of prints and drawings. The father is a fashionable don at Oxford. He teaches philosophy and publishes catchy articles in the *New York Review of Books*. Mother, a psychoanalyst. They know everybody; that's made clear when Max meets Camilla at the Kahns' Sunday lunch.

Camilla and Max go to his apartment directly from lunch. He still lives on Sparks Street, looking for something larger. Would she like a brandy? He puts a recording of *Dido and Aeneas* on the turntable, makes sure that she sits down on the sofa, where he can be beside her, and not on an armchair. His visits to England have been very brief. The way she talks is amusing. Is it the Oxford accent, or an abbreviated form of speech that's even more refined? At times, during lunch, he didn't understand what she was saying. He fiddles with the snifters, which are too large, and the bottle.

She says, Aren't you taking me to bed?

He has never made love like this before. There are no preliminaries. The borders that are crossed he would have thought were lifetimes away.

It's six o'clock. She picks up her clothes, urinates loudly leaving the bathroom door open, uses his toothbrush, and tells him she may be found in the telephone book.

He calls—the next day.

THE MARRIAGE to Camilla is contracted carelessly.

She loves gardens. The apartment on Highland Terrace

they move into, really the wing of a large house, belongs to the aged widow of a Medical School professor, a cousin of the Storrows. It has a brick-lined patio. Around it, beds where the widow's gardener has planted perennials. The widow agrees to give them a right of first refusal; as she has no intention of selling the house, it will be of use only when she dies. Camilla is very cheerful. She whistles when she is in the house, wears jeans and Max's worn-out shirts, and bicycles to the Fogg. She has replanted the handkerchief-sized garden. The gardener—initially skeptical—approves of the result, and weeds and waters when they are away. She is keeping the apartment very bare; Max has so many books one doesn't need anything except a bed. A bed they have. Other furniture arrives later. Max has never been so happy.

Camilla longs for the country. Her parents live in an ancient stone house, a half hour outside Oxford; that's how she was brought up. If they only had a place to get away to on weekends, and for at least a part of Max's lovely, long vacations. Of course, the Fogg remains open, but something can be worked out.

They have bought a Jaguar two-seater. With the top down, they explore the towns on the North Shore and also, with less confidence, the South Shore around Cohasset. It's dreadfully suburban; Dover would do, if it weren't so full of stuffy types who work for insurance companies or on State Street. Charlie Swan comes up with a solution: they must head farther west, to the Berkshires, where he owns a house in Billington. The way Camilla drives, they can be there in under two hours. He knows of just the property for them, on a hillside, across a narrow valley from his place, with a view straight into the sunset. The garden is a succession of terraces held up by old brick walls. They have, of course, seen a good deal of Charlie and Toby. Max never really lost contact with them after the meeting in Beijing; Camilla knows Charlie from Oxford and London. He and Toby come to Camilla and Max's wedding dinner, which is given by the Kahns.

Max buys the house Charlie has found. It's a ruin inside, but that's just as well because Camilla wants to change everything, and Charlie, who hasn't accepted a job of this sort in the last twenty years, offers to do the design work. It will be superb, a hymn to their friendship. Fortunately, a farmer's cottage comes with the house; it's in good condition, so that Camilla and Max can start their weekend existence immediately. Charlie is spending less time in Europe; he comes to Billington regularly. Both he and Toby are expert cooks. When they are only up for weekends, on Saturday nights, and more often when they are in residence, there is a big dinner at Charlie's. Naturally, they count on Camilla and Max. Max admires everything about Charlie's house: a brick Shaker structure, very spare but so graceful that it wears a smiling air of welcome. The collection of American furniture and bric-a-brac delights by its fantasy; a fitting extension, Max thinks, of the eccentric who coexists in Charlie with the rigorous bully. And Max likes Charlie's guests. They are a mixture of local patricians—stooped, bony men in tired tweeds or gabardine, depending on the season, whose wives have handshakes like lumberjacks—and collectible New Yorkers qualified by money, acknowledged talent, or extreme good looks. Max's new crowd. Charlie invites "my kind of queer" only: architects or artists and an occasional

beauty, like Toby. Except for a few old friends, sometimes referred to as "that adorable creature," about whose relation
to Charlie one might speculate this way or that, Max believes
sexual orientation is not a factor that determines Charlie's
favor. None of these men are special friends of Toby's. Who
are Toby's friends? When and where does he see them?

Toby joins Max and Camilla on their walks through the
woods at the other end of the valley. Sometimes Max and
Toby go rock climbing alone. Max thinks that Toby was right
when he worried about disappointing him. That is because
Max does feel that Toby has let him down. He is not making
progress along any road one can recognize. At work, he is
Charlie's man Friday, that's all. Charlie's nose is always in
some book; his library makes Max envious. Toby reads only
magazines. He is sweetness incarnate, but his conversation
has not been refurbished; one finds it dull. In a way, it is like
his looks—the beautiful face of an adolescent paired with
the body of a young man menaced by incipient thickness—
at the midriff, perceptible ever so slightly about the cheeks—
which is more dangerous than baby fat.

MAX KNOWS that many years have passed since a treatise
examining the intellectual foundations of contract law has
been published by a common law scholar. He thinks he can
write such a book—a short work, openly speculative in nature, free of academic jargon and the apparatus of footnotes.
The reconstruction of the house in Billington has reached a
stage at which it is quite possible to think of spending a sabbatical year there in comfort. He can imagine no place
where he would prefer to write—lifting his eyes from the

text to stare at the empty sky. Reference materials can be shipped to him by the Law School library as needed, or he will make quick expeditions to Cambridge. Camilla agrees; she has been urging Max to spread his wings. The Fogg is good about rearranging her schedule. She will need to spend only two nights each week at Highland Terrace. With the purchase of a Volvo station wagon, chosen despite Charlie's protest that its name and plum-red color make him think of a vulva, they become a two-car family. The book advances slowly, but Max grows fond of following his thoughts where they lead. The sentences he sets down on paper to express them seem becoming; he rejoices at each small success. When he rereads the text in the spring, he concludes that what he has done is worthy of being continued. He negotiates an indefinite extension of his leave. It occurs to him that he might dedicate his book to the memory of Cousin Emma as well as to Camilla. The former gave him the freedom to write in perfect conditions, the latter his new self-confidence.

WITH THE RETURN of good weather, the tempo of social activities quickens in Billington and the two adjoining towns where people who count are apt to have their houses. A short distance down the road from Max and Camilla's stands a bleak structure surrounded by yews. The Rookery, for that is the name on the owners' notepaper under an embossed crown, is the dwelling of the elderly Lord and Lady Howe. The baron—the third to have the title—descends from a man who grew rich grinding wheat into flour. He is an ornithologist married to an American. Her family made uniforms for the army in a nearby town where rich people no longer live. From late June until early September, the Rookery is the scene of festivities equal to Charlie's in their standing and power of attraction. The food comes out of a can or the freezer, but it is served by the English butler, one dresses for dinner, and the women withdraw to have coffee in the pink drawing room that has the same view as Max's study. Through their mothers, Camilla and Lord Howe are cousins. The Rookery becomes the other pole of Camilla and Max's evening and weekend life. No disloyalty to Charlie is involved: he is constantly at the Howes', and the titled couple is in the place of honor when Charlie and Toby entertain. By now Max finds it only natural that the friendship between Charlie and Ricky Howe predates by many years Charlie's decision to buy a house in the Billington valley. He shares the general regret that exigencies of their schedule prevent the Howes from staying in the valley until the foliage hits its reddest peak in October.

Among the Howes' houseguests is Roland Cartwright, famous for filming the war in Vietnam and Laos. Great face, like a menhir. His departures from the Rookery are unpredictable, influenced by summonses from producers and backers in Los Angeles and New York. He returns with tales of deals that were almost made. Another relentlessly English voice at the table, but different in range and color: while Camilla and Ricky are laconic, their enthusiasms a jolly mumble, this man's diction is a compendium of Dickens and the Rolling Stones. It's lucky that Roland and Charlie are both so amusing: otherwise, when Charlie decides he also wants to be heard, the noise would be intolerable. Roland has shot films everywhere—including a feature in Greece. That's where he perfected for Camilla the world-famous four-hour Cartwright tour of Athens. The visits to the Acropolis and the Archeological Museum were quite thorough, and yet they had time to eat broiled fish in a taverna in Piraeus before she took the evening plane for London. It comes as a surprise to Max that Camilla had traveled in Greece with Roland, but how much can one learn of anyone's life? They had met on the site of a dig, where she was writing up labels for shards of pottery and he was filming a scene.

In spite of his efforts, Roland is temporarily unable to conclude a movie deal. A position might open in the film department of Boston University or MIT, perhaps a specially funded program. He takes to going into town with Camilla. The Volvo is a great help, because it can hold the gear Roland is obliged to pack. He stays in the guest room at Highland Terrace. Sometimes Camilla leaves him there if his business is not concluded during the three-day stint in Cambridge and brings him back to Billington the following week. It's much less spooky for her to go back to a flat in which one finds signs of human life. The health of the widow in the other part of the house is sinking. According to the gardener, she hardly leaves her bed. A visiting nurse comes at night to spell the cook and the maid.

ON THE FOURTH OF JULY, Charlie sprains his back playing tennis in the club tournament. The pain is agonizing and spreads to his left leg and then one arm. The pope of lower-back doctors in New York recommends an operation to relieve the pressure on the nerve of damaged and eroded disks. Charlie won't hear of it; he dislikes cutting and sewing when it's his own skin. The alternative remedy is rest and, later, when the pain has receded, exercises to be performed lying on the floor. Charlie's design for a new museum in Rotterdam has won an international competition. The project is fully funded, so that work can begin at once. Fortunately, the next phase is engineering and detailed drawings: these are matters that do not require his presence either in the New York office or on the site. Work conferences can be held around the oak table in his study in Billington; draftsmen's tables are set up on the glassed-in back veranda. Toby's reaction causes an unexpected difficulty, which Charlie doesn't know how to overcome. Charlie speaks about it to Max, seeking his counsel. Perhaps he hopes that Max will intercede with the boy. It appears that Toby doesn't want to remain in Billington with Charlie during this period when people from the office will be streaming in, because he doesn't want them to think that he is Charlie's "wife," looking after him at home. But he doesn't want to return to the office in New York either. There is nothing for him to do in that place; he has always been with Charlie, at his beck and call, and without Charlie there, he will be visibly useless, the target of office jokes. Max points out to Toby that merely proves his job, at which he is badly needed, is in Billington, helping Charlie to review papers and manage the telephone. Toby is obdurate. He doesn't need me here for work either, he insists; let him get someone he thinks is qualified.

Max sees that he will not be able to pull a rabbit out of the hat for his old friend. There's a problem with Toby, he tells Charlie, you've been treating him like a precocious child, and now he thinks he's grown out of that role. You'll have to let him fend for himself and find his own place in life, even if you don't like what he finds.

Charlie answers: I can't bear to be without Toby. How sharper than a serpent's tooth! I will die.

Of course, he doesn't. August strikes the Berkshires like a drum. Every bungalow on the Stockbridge Bowl, every converted barn, has been rented. Outside the Morpheus Arms Motel, the NO VACANCY sign flashes red with pride. Busloads of tourists scavenge for antiques and last year's maple syrup; they invest the lawn at Tanglewood. Charlie refuses to have people from his office or the consulting engineer's live at his house. Those who have not been nimble enough to find accommodations with a friend arrive in two vans at nine-thirty in the morning and leave by four. Charlie won't work any later. Every weekday, Max spends the late afternoon at Charlie's. He swims first, while Charlie is still taking his nap, and then they talk and drink wine in the heavy shade of a red beech. Since Toby's departure, Charlie has stopped having people to dinner. He claims that it's too much work, too hard on his back, even though the Polish couple who look after the house customarily wait on the table and wash the dishes. He wouldn't dream of letting that woman cook food for human consumption. So Max drives Charlie over to the Howes', when they give a dinner there, or the van Lenneps'. Claire van Lennep is French and still good-looking; it's a relief from the swill served by Lady Howe to eat at her house. Otherwise, Charlie makes pasta, just for the two of them, and some salad. If the program at Tanglewood is especially enticing they go to hear one piece. Charlie's back still can't endure an entire concert.

THE THING IS that Camilla is replacing two colleagues at the Fogg who simply had to take holidays in August, and the poor thing is working a full-time schedule. There is so much clerical stuff to catch up on that the work spills over into the weekend; in spite of the heat, it's really easier to stay in Cambridge for the weekend as well than to fight the turnpike traffic, first to the country and then back to town. Roland has landed the job at Boston University. He is preparing his course. He too needs to be in town. There has been a wave of burglaries in Cambridge. Max suggests that the arrangement whereby Roland spends most of his nights at Highland Terrace be made official: he can be their tenant, so long as Max is on leave. The house-sitting in itself will suffice as rent, and he can make an occasional present to the cleaning lady. She adores him anyway. With Roland's position comes the funding for a course assistant. He hires an overjoyed Toby. That's better from Charlie's point of view than any other solution, short of having Toby remain with him, which, for the time being, seems impossible: at least he knows more or less where Toby is and what he is doing. But Toby refuses to become the other house sitter at Highland Terrace. Don't try to trap me, he says when the suggestion is made. He gets a one-room studio, a fuckpad Charlie calls it, near Symphony Hall. The answering machine's recorded announcement is,

If you recognize my voice, you've got the right number. Don't feel obliged to leave a message.

On Friday afternoon of the Labor Day weekend, the Volvo deposits Toby at Charlie's and Roland at the Howes'. Through the window of his study, which is open, Max hears the wheels on the unpaved road and sees the car speed toward the Rookery. More than an hour passes. Camilla has not returned; she has not called. Max's impatience gives way to nervous unease. A paralyzing timidity, not unmixed with shame, of a sort he has not felt in years, makes his body stiff and achy. He cannot accomplish any of the gestures he knows would be automatic in other circumstances—but what are the present circumstances? He does not telephone Camilla at the Howes' or bicycle to their house. When the car returns, he listens to its doors slam and Camilla's footsteps on the drive and then on the stair, remaining frozen in the chair at his desk until Camilla stands in the door, calling his name.

Are you cross because I stayed too long at Ricky's?

Did you? I had no idea, of course I'm not.

Will she believe that he has been hard at work on his book, his vaunted concentration unbroken? Ostensibly, that is the point of the game he is playing, but he doesn't mean to be believed. He wants her to know that he feels wounded but won't discuss it. In the meantime, he gets her bags and carries them to the bedroom. Her dress is like a sleeveless blue nightgown with horizontal red stripes. When she takes it off she is bare except for her sandals. She stoops to untie them. At once, Max wants her. Two weeks have passed since they last slept together. She pushes him away: it's some sort of mushroom inside her, like yeast. Perhaps the heat brought it on, the doctor doesn't know. She is to let it heal.

Now it's impossible to retreat. He whispers, asking for a service she usually performs so willingly.

Poorest noodle, I can't; not until I am all well. If you make me I will like it, and I'll get all wet inside.

It's the evening of the Howes' annual dance. Notables from small islands in Maine and Adirondack camps, and titled persons summoned from more remote foreign villeggiaturas occupy every guest room at the Rookery. The overflow has been billeted, according to rank, with the Howes' indigenous friends. They have let Max off the hook, because poor Camilla won't be back from Cambridge until the last minute, and it's well known that he can't cope.

Camilla is in the tub, soaking. His own preparations finished, Max watches her from the distance of the washbasin on which he is perching. She asks him to scrub her back with the loofah and explains how she had some gins with Roland and Ricky while they watched the band set up. Then she and Roland had a dip in the pond. Such a lovely swim; no chlorine to hurt my pussy.

The gumshoe inside Max is on the case. Of course, when she threw it on the bed, her bikini was dry. They swam naked. But why get excited over that, chump? He checks her oil every night, in your own bed in Highland Terrace! Get the picture? No, Max doesn't. He will walk out from this B-grade movie. Roland is too old for Camilla; besides, hasn't Charlie said he is another one of those English queers? If he is banging anyone, it's Ricky Howe or Toby. Give Sam Spade his check and a tip in cash, and send him home. He is very tender with Camilla, while she is dressing, during the dinner at Charlie's, and later when she presses her body against his on the dance floor under the green-and-white Saracen tent. Her tongue is in his mouth. He moves his arm a little, so that his fingers can feel the tuft under her arm. Yes, she is sweating. The tongue withdraws. She blows into his ear, very hot, and whispers, Bugger my yeast!

They will leave for Cambridge late on Monday evening right after dinner—Camilla, Roland, and Toby—just as they came. Camilla will drive. She always manages to stay sober.

And what a nice dinner Charlie has put together that Monday! The Howes' guests have departed or have found other distractions, so it's just the little clan and the van Lenneps. This is something of a promotion for them: Charlie needs compulsively the company of beautiful women. Since Camilla has been away so much, he has had Claire van Lennep help him arrange flowers and has discovered how well she reads aloud in French. Ricky has brought some great red wine. No use drinking it at home, the food is too awful, he explains. Charlie's back is better, but Toby has prepared the main dish anyway—a Lebanese chicken couscous, with lots of mint and coriander. It's like old times, but no one says so. Instead, they talk about Beirut and what a hopeless mess it has become. Toby's father now lives in Cairo. Why couldn't they all go to Egypt at Christmas? He could organize their Nile trip; according to Edwina Howe, it's only worth doing if one charters a boat with a crew that doesn't smell like spoiled mutton. The van Lenneps make no comment. Max thinks it's too bad, the trip is probably beyond their means. But Edwina cries out, Toby darling, do call your father. Of course, it is five in the morning in Egypt and the dear boy has vanished from the room; by the time he returns, they are talking of other things. Max observes that his face is flushed—from the sun or from the stove—and his hairline has receded. Is his hair thinner as well, or does it just look that way because he has allowed it to grow long?

As the others say good-bye, Max tells Charlie he will stay for a nightcap. They move to the porch and drink brandy. A waning moon hangs in the sky. The lights of Max's house can be seen on the other side of the valley, lonely but vivid. Only the outside lanterns are on at the Howes'. Charlie begins to cry, and from time to time keens a little. Max leaves his chair, sits down beside Charlie on the sofa, and puts his arm around his shoulders. Shush, he says. He will be back soon.

That is not why I am crying. I am crying because I have hardened my heart against him.

After a while, the sobbing stops, and Max removes his arm.

What do you mean? he asks.

I am mourning the death of love. It's that which I mind, not his going away, not anymore. When he is away, there are hours upon hours each day when I don't think of him at all. Intermissions of the heart.

Then Charlie adds, Did you look at his eyes? He is on drugs again. That's why he had to leave the table.

Les très riches heures . . . Abruptly, vacations end for grown-ups as well as children. Charlie feels completely fit. He decides to return to New York and work as before. When Toby tells him that he would like to stay on in Boston rather than take back the old job in Charlie's firm, Charlie responds with great calm. The opportunity to learn about film is not to be missed, Roland is an artist, Toby should think of Billington as his weekend home. He is to bring friends if he likes, just make sure they don't piss on the bathroom floor. To Max he remarks, I know I won't see him if he has to take the bus. That's why I am giving him the jeep and putting it in his name. The parking tickets will be his too.

The University Press has sent Max's manuscript to colleagues in the United States and England for comments. He is to some degree surprised, at first, and then overwhelmed by the warmth and admiration they express. The dean asks Max to think of resuming teaching during the spring semester. The book seems ready for publication, and even if Max wishes to polish certain passages there is ample time for that before Christmas. Max feels that, possibly for the first time, the Law School considers his presence on the faculty justified by something other than successful completion of the academic obstacle course and standard good behavior. He accepts the dean's suggestion gratefully. Shortly afterward, upon the retirement of the revered incumbent, Max becomes the fifth Elijah Wooden Professor of Jurisprudence. Camilla congratulates Max on acceding to such a distinguished chair and hurts his feelings: she giggles that the name fits him to a T.

Roland has an apartment off Central Square. The neighborhood is on the raffish side. He has had to install bars in the windows and attach an iron pole to the front door. At the end of the pole is a hook that enters an eyebolt screwed into the floor. The point is to buttress the door against neighbors who might wish to kick it in. In the circumstances, Max thinks Roland was very good to move out of Highland Terrace so promptly. Not that there is much to worry about so far as Roland's personal safety is concerned. He has acquired a used Harley-Davidson and dresses in black jeans, black boots, and a leather jacket. One can't distinguish him from the local hoods.

Boston attracts visiting Brits like flypaper. The wardens of Oxford and Cambridge colleges lodge with the president of Harvard or in the Houses; luminaries of popular culture manage as best they can. Max notes their tribal aversion to hotels. The spare bedroom at Highland Terrace, Max's study, and the vast couches in the living room afford nights of healthful slumber to a series of men and women of all ages, friends of Camilla's, her parents', or Roland's, related to celebrated writers and politicians, and quite garrulous at breakfast. The world is so very small; that's what they keep repeating. Roland organizes the dinners: these are protracted affairs at his place with no defined point of beginning or end. The music is brutally loud. One eats ribs from a soul restaurant next door, Thai soup, and *pappadum*. Max thinks it's the last place on the eastern seaboard where adults smoke pot. Toby reinforces that view. They often sit side by side at these parties. It's nice to know they go back a long way. Occasionally, Toby brings along a third-year law student from Boston University, who is taking Roland's course not for credit. He is a shy fellow, with glasses and an oddly tight, muscular body. Max and he discuss affirmative action cases, which are all the rage, and this boy Mike is studying in his constitutional law class. Toby asks Max to vouch for Mike to Charlie before Mike's first visit to Billington.

It's not always easy for Max to interrupt his work in order to accompany Camilla to Roland's parties—there seems to be one every evening—and it's harder still to remain until they end. Camilla loves to stay up. Of course, she doesn't need to be at the Fogg until eleven, whereas he teaches a nine o'clock class. Fortunately, she doesn't mind if he doesn't go or sneaks away early. He leaves her the car. At that hour, it's easy to catch a taxi at Central Square, and not particularly dangerous.

THE REVIEWS OF Max's book are extravagantly favorable. What's more, they appear in the principal newspapers and magazines of general circulation, not only in legal journals. He is told that he may have a best-seller on his hands. Toward the end of the semester, Max is asked to do a cover article on the crisis over racial quotas for the Sunday *Times Magazine*. The deadline is tight. He has no experience with this sort of writing and finds it difficult to lay out his arguments in the space he has been given. Obliged to work late, he realizes that at three or four in the morning Camilla is still at Roland's. The following night he makes himself wake up nearly every hour to fix the hour of her return. By the time the garage door opens and then slams shut, the sun has risen. One evening when she goes out, hot with shame he opens the box in which she keeps her diaphragm. It's empty. Over the next several weeks he repeats the act he loathes each times she goes out alone. The result is the same. Finally, he puts a scrap of paper where the diaphragm should be. On it he has written, "With whom are you using it?" She is still asleep the next morning when he leaves for the Law School. Since it is rare for her to be back from the Fogg before six, he does not hurry home. But she is there when he returns, preparing dinner. He wonders what to expect. With Kate, he fought constantly. Camilla and he have never quarreled. She accepts the gin he offers and asks, Didn't your mother tell you never to touch other people's belongings?

Of course.

How right she was. I wear it every night, to find out whether I am allergic to it or something else is wrong.

So that's it. He apologizes and half-believes she has told the truth. They do not refer to the incident again.

MEMORIAL DAY WEEKEND approaches and so does the Harvard commencement. Camilla must stay in town. There is so much to do. The Fogg is preparing a special event for the overseers and the committee to visit the Fine Arts Department. Max asks if she will mind his going to Billington without her; he has an unpleasant premonition of stagnant Cambridge heat, his own drowsiness as he grades examination papers, hours to be spent in the evenings waiting for Camilla to return from the museum, and telephone calls from noisy restaurants somewhere in the North End. I am stuck here eating the most dreadful pizza. Will you be an angel? Jump in the car and join us. No? Roland will take me home then, on his bike.

Camilla won't mind in the least. In that case, he will return only in time for the commencement, when it's his duty to march in the academic procession as the Wooden Profes-

sor. Toby telephones. He is sick with an unpleasant summer
flu, too groggy to drive. Can Max give him a ride? They get a
late start. On the turnpike, Max lets the Jaguar soar. He
hasn't had a speeding ticket in years. To hell with it, if he is
caught. The night is his time of day: black solitude, enchant-
ment. He glances at Toby. The boy is asleep with his mouth
open. A while later, Toby wakes up. He asks Max to stop the
car. They both urinate by the side of the road, in the amber
nimbus of the parking light. Onward. Max keeps the car
stereo very low, so they can talk. Toby tells him he has seen
his father; he came to Boston with his new wife, a Lebanese
Muslim who has been to college in Mount Holyoke. Not
much older than Toby, but a funny throwback to the fifties.
Plucked eyebrows, shiny brown hair done up in curls and
sprayed to stay put like a wedding cake, skin soft and creamy,
perhaps because she is too plump, lots of rings, and these in-
credibly correct clothes. Everything on her matches the yellow blouse or the fingernails, and it all comes from Hermès.
The new deal is Toby gets an allowance from a trust—so
much per month, enough to live the way he lives now and
pay medical insurance. Just don't call Papa; if he wants to be
in touch, he'll call you. Boy, were they ever worried about
insurance! Is there some way I can sue to get some of his real
money? I'm the only child—so far.

Not until he dies, Max tells him.

No way. He'll just keep eating halvah and shrivel.

Toby dozes off again. When he wakes, he tells Max he is
scared. The job with Roland is just lugging equipment
around and working the projector. Maybe the kids get something out of it, like a diploma to clip to a résumé. Who will

want to hire an assistant to a guy teaching about film? He doesn't see Roland ever making a film again; he's gotten too weird, out of touch. He should have followed Charlie's advice: go to Cooper Union or Pratt, learn the basics, become a designer. Charlie is the only one who thinks about his future.

It's not too late, Max assures him. Charlie can get anyone into the program, even this late in the year. He asks whether the allowance from the trust will cover tuition and the cost of living in New York. Toby replies that if the school will take him he supposes he can work for Charlie part-time, maybe even stay with him. The vision of Charlie's happiness when he learns that this is what the boy wants is so intense that Max decides to say nothing more about it. The boy might think he is walking into a trap. Instead, he inquires about Toby's mother. She too is a part of the trust. Enough to pay for her and a nurse for life.

AFTERNOON of Commencement Day. Sky absolutely spotless, as though it had been washed down. Max heads for Highland Terrace, slightly tipsy from the rum punch served in the Harkness Quadrangle for Law School students and their parents. Shouldn't drink the stuff on an empty stomach, but the buffet reeks of mayonnaise and tuna. Horror of horrors! One of Max's own classmates is in the crowd on the lawn. Now that the classmate has explained it, the reason for his presence becomes clear—even plausible. He has a son, who was moreover in a class that Max taught; of course, Max failed to connect the son with the parent. Yes, the proud father explains, he had the boy in the second year of college! One wife, one child, and one house. The classmate laughs.

He works in the mortgage loan section of a Hartford insurance company. Serves him right. He must have used that one-wife line one thousand times. At home, Camilla is waiting in the cool shade of the garden. She serves Max a glass of iced tea with mint. With her, there are really no preliminaries: she is leaving for London; there is a post at the National Gallery she can't possibly turn down. He absorbs the news, and also the realization that she is not asking whether he might be willing to move to London as well, to be with her.

Camilla observes him as he stares at the wisteria, which has begun to bloom. He is red in the face, but that's from the heat. Already he has pushed the resentment down into his gut, where it will rot like a field mouse in a snake. His fingers lie quiet and flat on the glass table. She averts her eyes. When she looks again, she sees that he has fallen asleep.

SHE DEPARTS next week, just as she had moved into the old Sparks Street apartment, with one large, heavy suitcase sufficient to contain all her paraphernalia—the blue jeans of which she takes such excellent care, velvet skirts in many shades of pastel, little-girl long dresses, wool socks, and underwear rolled up in tiny balls—bending under its weight until Max wrestles it from her hand and lifts it into the trunk of a waiting taxi. Everything else remains with Max: the see-through birdhouse outside the upstairs bedroom window, disaffected while its clientele feeds off the summer's bounty, the marks left by cigarettes burning at the edge of the Chinese Chippendale coffee table, a profusion of arrangements Max thinks he has neither the energy to undo nor the science to continue.

Later that summer the quickie divorce comes through. They meet at the office of the lawyer who handles Max's trust. When the papers have been signed, she holds out her hand to Max and then her cheek, which he kisses.

We have given our hearts away, a sordid boon! are her parting words.

V

MY DEPARTED tenants' spoors are everywhere, I complained to Charlie. Such odd people. They have lined all the drawers! White linoleum, with red strawberries! Not just here, in the kitchen, but even the bureau drawers. In my bedroom, all through the house. Look: a vegetable juice machine! An electric knife sharpener and a wall bracket for the Dustbuster! The thing itself is in the pantry, plugged into the outlet, gathering force. You can hear it breathing. Do you suppose someday they will drive up to the door, use the set of keys they forgot to return, and take away all these gadgets? Come to think of it, these aren't really spoors, they're more like abandoned pets! What people do when they leave a rented house at the end of the summer—a dog tied to the cherry tree so he won't make them feel bad as he races after the car.

We were having a cup of tea at the kitchen table. I had returned to Billington for the first time after two years' absence from the house and from Charlie.

AFTER THE DIVORCE, my principal sensation was embarrassment: the near certitude that she had made a fool of me.

Hiding would be easier, I supposed, in Cambridge than during weekends in Billington. Fortunately, the real estate agent—contacted on my behalf by Charlie—quickly found a best-selling writer eager to rent the Billington house from year to year. His real goal was to buy a place in the valley; if my present mood continued, why wouldn't I, in time, sell my property to him? On his side, the package deal included a wife, seemingly ready to keep up the garden, and two small children with turned-up noses. I liked thinking about the children; they would learn to swim in my swimming pool, and later on in the year, zipped up in snowsuits, matching knitted ski hats on their heads, they would slide down the meadow on my Flying Eagle sled. I had been careful to point out its presence in the garage. The picture was rather like what I might have imagined for the issue Camilla's birth control device had stopped in its tracks.

Toby was in Cambridge during the summer of my divorce, hanging out, as he put it. We saw each other often. I would find him waiting in the kitchen when I came home from my office at Langdell. He would have prepared a surprise, one of the recipes for sherbets and Italian ices he was always trying out. Sometimes the Cambridge heat was so heavy that, instead of eating the surprise in the garden, we turned on the air-conditioning and took refuge inside. We talked about Camilla nostalgically, as though we had known her very long ago; I assumed he wanted to comfort me without letting his purpose appear. Pratt had indeed accepted him as a special student; he would be working for Charlie part-time. But he wasn't planning to live with Charlie. When his allowance and salary were put together, there seemed to be enough to pay for a place of his own, yet another studio walk-up.

My mother was the last—perhaps the only—person to whom I had written and telephoned regularly, without a specific reason. My other correspondence has all been in the thank you and recommendation for a job or for a grant category. I have never known how to "keep up" on the telephone. It was, therefore, no surprise to realize that I had again lost touch with Charlie. For all the bluster about my being an object of his predilection, Charlie was equally silent and absent. Our friendship seemed to have retreated to its previous place in the limbo of insignificant connections, with one difference so far as I was concerned: whereas previously I had expected nothing from him, I now feared that in future dealings I would have to come to terms with habits and expectations that the Billington context and Camilla's presence had created. That was a pity.

My other link to Billington and Camilla was also severed at the end of that summer by a departure, but more comically and in circumstances I could not easily put out of my mind. Boston University had not renewed Roland's teaching appointment. Neither he nor Camilla nor even Toby had mentioned that setback, although, since one of its consequences was that Toby likewise had lost his job, it must have weighed in Toby's decision to prepare himself at Pratt for another career. Roland finally told me about it, when he appeared at Highland Terrace late one afternoon with various household utensils he had borrowed from Camilla and wished to return. He was going back to England, to look into some British Arts Council opening that sounded promising. Would I like to have his motorcycle? He wasn't taking it along. A large lump of spite directed at Roland had built up inside me, and I was tempted to turn him down brutally. On the other hand, quite irrationally, I didn't want this last meeting to end quite so soon. I reconsidered, and said that if I tried it out and found I could handle such a powerful machine I would buy it.

No, I mean to give it to you. You have been very patient and very kind as well.

I said it would have to be a purchase. As I had expected, he didn't put up much of a fight.

Later, over pizza at Camilla's favorite restaurant in the North End—we went there on the Harley-Davidson to test, under Roland's supervision, my ability to drive it in Boston traffic—when we were well into the second bottle of a Piedmont wine, I put the question. Had he been sleeping with Camilla?

No, or rather, yes. Once or twice, years ago, even longer ago than Greece. Greek prehistory. He laughed.

And here?

Never. By the time I thought of it, she was banging Toby. Mad about him. An experiment that didn't work. I suppose no harm in your knowing it now.

During the winter that followed, I rode my motorcycle to Langdell and to dinner parties in Cambridge and Boston, at which I was once again the object of attention deriving from considerations other than my professorial eminence. It was just as well that the machine amused me. My pleasant habit of walking after dark across the Common and on Brattle Street had become dangerous. Knifings, attacks with fists and boots, and bullet wounds now frequently accompanied transactions I used to think of as having essentially a financial nature—the surrender of the contents of one's wallet to young men in urgent need of cash. In her bedroom, on the second story of a Brattle Street house, too terrified to cry out, the adolescent daughter of friends had been raped while the parents calmly dined downstairs. Had she screamed and been heard, what would my colleague, a small and gentle man, have done? I asked myself. If he had tried to fight off the aggressor, should one not imagine a scene of even greater horror: the wounded father forced to look on as the mother as well as the daughter were sodomized, mutilated, and killed? My bedridden landlady's presence in the main part of the house, the comings and goings of her nurses, whose car wheels on the driveway gravel made a shrieking noise in the taut night silence of Highland Terrace, did nothing to reassure me. I thought these women were a magnet for violence, predestined victims of unspeakable butchery into which I would somehow be drawn. It seemed grotesque to install bars in my windows—the widow had not done it— or an electric alarm system. I was too fond of sleeping with my window open; besides, weren't those contraptions apt to begin to whine because of a dip or surge in the electric current?

Visiting Austin, to chair a symposium at the University of Texas, I almost succumbed to temptation: buy a revolver and twenty rounds of ammunition at a shopping mall, put them in a garment bag I would check in at the airport, and transport the cache to Cambridge. At least the odds would be more or less even in a fight to the death—gun against gun, and not my helpless, naked body against theirs, bleeding in my bed or eviscerated by the intruders on the floor of a closet in which I had been cowering. Fear of luggage being X-rayed, and the scandal that would ensue, stopped me. I rode my motorcycle to the police station in Central Square and held my temper until the administrative procedures were completed and I became the owner of a legally registered Glock pistol. Death! I was in possession of an instrument of death! Death of others and my own as well, commanded by my will, ending my loneliness and fatigue, bringing prosperity to rejoicing orphans in Alabama. That is what reposed in the bottom compartment of my cylindrical night table, a place intended for a chamber pot, one which, as I had no such vessel, my maid never opened. But was my gun in working order? I would go down to the cellar, put on gloves to prevent powder marks, fire bullet after bullet at the earth and boulder wall, then take the piece apart and, having oiled and assembled it carefully, return it to its place. And always the question remained: Will it let me down the next time?

In the spring I applied for a leave. The Wooden professorship is like a Russian doll inside which is a series of other dolls, identical to the first but diminishing in size. Among its delights, revealed to me one by one, was the renewal, on the date I became the incumbent, of the sabbatical cycle. It was my right, once again, to be absent for a year! My Chinese friends had not forgotten me. I was ceremoniously invited to teach at Beijing University and thus found myself with a front-row seat from which to observe and mourn the events of May and June '89.

★   ★   ★

I WAS DESCRIBING the Tiananmen spring to Charlie. The words came with difficulty. How could I convey the good humor of my students, their delight in interminable hours of talk and their unabashed affection for each other? It was as though the memories of what they and their families had suffered during the Cultural Revolution—and all my students were old enough to have such memories—had only reinforced their optimism. Sometimes I allowed myself to think that their secret might be that they truly were able to believe in the eventual victory of the good over the bad, but I realized at the same time that my notions of good and evil corresponded with theirs only approximately, so that perhaps what really sustained them was the conviction that in the end they could not be stopped from changing China. It was even harder to speak of the hurt caused by the massacre, their astonishment that such a thing could have happened. Some literally disappeared—fled Beijing. Many of those less seriously implicated quickly went into hiding, taking refuge behind a wall of others who wished them well—family, friends, workers, and in the case of one of my junior colleagues, an entire Chinese army unit with whom he and his wife, a military history researcher, happened to share barracks. The unit simply refused the police access to him. Many lessons in solidarity had apparently been learned during the Mao years.

I made more tea. He put his pad of graph paper on his knee and wrote the list of changes I wanted to make in the house. They had a common theme: I wanted to be at the hub of a wheel, a man living in a large house organized for him alone. What I meant, of course, was that I did not want to live there without Camilla as though Camilla were still present.

Charlie used a thick, old-fashioned fountain pen. I admired his angular draftsman's script, a promise of sketches and elevations we would pore over together.

These are problems that Toby should be able to handle, he announced. I will send him over tomorrow. Their solution will consecrate your friendship.

I didn't think Charlie would redo my house to celebrate a divorce as well as a marriage, so I had been waiting for something like this and wasn't sure whether I wanted to object. In the event, I didn't. Instead I asked, rather flatly I thought, about Toby's progress at Pratt.

He is gifted, very imaginative, quite as I had foretold. He has worked hard. Alas, as you will see at dinner tonight, in other ways he isn't in top form. That is why I have suggested that he spend the summer in Billington, and not in the office. Has that added to his malaise? I am not sure, but I am glad to find a project he can do here. Let friendship and art combine! Come early. We will watch the sunset. You and Toby will talk while I take care of last-minute chopping and stirring.

There are almost never mosquitoes in Charlie's garden, the hillside being swept by breezes, but Toby preferred to sit on the screened porch. He wore a thin cashmere sweater the color of a pale green melon and particularly luxurious silk trousers. The puffiness of his face, the slight layer of fat about to turn into a second chin, which I had thought were going to coarsen his face, had disappeared. His features looked chiseled, even more finely than when I first saw him, stronger and nobler. It didn't matter that his hair had receded; he must have come to think so himself, because he wore it very short now, making no effort to conceal the onset of baldness. He had adopted Charlie's Roman style. I was moved by his beauty.

Roland stopped in New York in January, on his way to the West Coast. He told me that you know. I am very sorry. It shouldn't have happened. I wish he hadn't talked. What was the use?

I had not expected him to speak of Camilla, certainly not so abruptly, as soon as we were alone.

It doesn't matter now, I replied. But you are right to bring it up.

You were angry, though. That's why you went off the air.

No, I was in another compartment of my existence, one where you and Charlie never set foot. Does he know? Did he know at the time?

He figured it out. He felt very bad and very bitter, for himself and for you. It was harder for him than when I am with another guy. You probably find that strange.

I admitted that I didn't understand.

He held out his hand. Come on, shake my hand. She would have left you anyway.

I took the hand. What else was there to do? He was right, Camilla had not left me because of him, that much was clear even to me and picking a quarrel wouldn't repair the indignity of having been cuckolded by a little fruit. Besides, I liked him. The droll side of the situation, that Charlie and I should be the two wronged husbands, was something I could savor.

I said, You had better tell Charlie that it's all in the open now.

Oh, yes. He advised me to talk to you. He thinks it would be hard to remain friends otherwise.

I knew that Edwina and Ricky Howe were coming to dinner. It would have annoyed me to think that they too had been in the audience, giggling at our misadventures, and I said so to Toby.

I don't know what they may have guessed, or what Camilla or Roland told them. Charlie and I never talked to them about it.

So that was that. I would have to study the Howes' behavior, attentive to excessive solicitude. Irony was not in the cards. They would have considered it ill bred.

Toby came to my house the next morning, with a schoolbag containing his own graph-paper pads and high-tech pens. He had studied Charlie's notes and thought about them. Charlie was right, the boy had talent, and he had obviously been learning the business: as we went from room to room, he gave visual form to my wishes, even those that were still vague and contradictory. Certain projects, which I had told Charlie I felt strongly about—redesigning the garden, making a new kitchen—he responded to coolly, suggesting, as though he had not noticed the self-pity and pique of which they were the expression, that they should be postponed, or perhaps given up altogether. When we had finished the tour, I told him I felt I was in good hands. That was the truth; especially as I didn't doubt that Charlie would keep an eye on the work.

It was warm for the end of June in the Berkshires, and I had been heating the swimming pool to spa temperature since I arrived. I asked Toby if he wanted to have a swim before we both went to lunch with Charlie. We tested the water. There was a layer of steam over the surface.

Go ahead, he said, I'll wait for you. I've been feeling lousy; now all of a sudden I am very tired. Charlie thinks I should go to New York to see another doctor.

TIMES HAD CHANGED. Some days later, having agreed with Toby on the work program, I left for a holiday in Europe, which was to begin at the Rumorosa. The invitation had been issued by Edna Joyce herself; she had written and then telephoned twice, to urge me to stay for two weeks and longer, if I could, and above all to make sure I was coming. Arthur would be there during a part of my visit and so would Laura. I had not seen Laura since Arthur and I visited her house on the hill overlooking Belluno, but we had parted and, I hoped, remained on good terms, even though I had written to her only a few times. The last letter was to tell her I was about to be married. Meanwhile, my relationship with Arthur had soured. I had introduced him to Camilla at the first opportunity; she was already living with me at Sparks Street and prepared the dinner. They each talked a blue streak—but only at me, as though making sure it was about people the other didn't know. During lunch the next day, Arthur infuriated me by announcing point-blank, without having been asked to express an opinion, You would do well to find a place of her own for that English girl; she's not for you.

Camilla was equally direct. Don't let him come here again. He's not my kind of pansy.

When I protested that he wasn't gay at all, she looked at me pityingly and said that I knew nothing about such things, and that anyway it didn't matter whether he was or wasn't.

I don't understand much about English attitudes. At the time, I understood even less. I did think, though, and have continued to believe, that the clash between those two was oddly unconnected to the disagreeable futility of the conversation at dinner or to Arthur's sexual orientation. I wondered if Arthur's being a Jew was not the more relevant element.

My respect for Arthur's shrewdness was considerable, so his remark about Camilla rankled, especially as he did nothing to withdraw it even after I announced, in due course, that I was marrying her. Nevertheless, I continued to see him, usually without her, until our divorce. Then I began to find it quite intolerable that he should have been so right, and all through the winter that preceded my sabbatical in China I was careful to avoid him, returning calls and leaving messages only when I thought he would be out, inventing reasons why all my lunches and dinners were spoken for. When Edna told me that I would be seeing him I was surprised, though I shouldn't have been, and, almost immediately, I realized that the prospect was not unpleasant. Then came the conversation with Toby about Camilla. He had indeed cleared the air. I realized that I would be thinking about Camilla less and less, and it had become possible to feel frankly cheerful about renewing the friendship with Arthur.

I returned to Billington at the end of August, in time for

the celebration of Charlie's sixtieth birthday. My house looked entirely ready. The huge sum I had agreed to spend had bought speed. Attractive young workmen apologized for not having removed all their tools and stepladders; others, like lepidopterists, bottles of Fantastik and rolls of paper towel in hand, were chasing scuff marks on doors and floorboards. My own inspection completed, I dialed Charlie's number to congratulate and thank Toby. A woman whose voice I didn't know answered the telephone. Toby was unavailable; I could speak to Charlie in a moment. My satisfaction would give Toby great joy, he told me, perhaps an important psychological lift. Of course, both Toby and he had seen the finished work, and I would have to forgive Toby for not inspecting it with me. But he, Charlie, wanted to see me before the evening's party. Could he come over within the next two hours?

I had landed in Boston the previous day, and had slept at Highland Terrace before setting out for the Berkshires, so I was fully rested. Nevertheless, I was experiencing, as always when I return home from a distant place, a sense of not having fully arrived, a sort of momentary estrangement for everything that should be most familiar. It's a sensation that sharpens the power of observation; when Charlie appeared, it made me take note of the change in him. A change, but since when? The beginning of the summer? That other, earlier summer when Camilla left me? I would have been unable to say with confidence. And what did it consist of? Fatigue, an appearance of distraction, certainly entered into it. After we had embraced—Charlie had taken to kissing me even in public—and I had wished him happy birthday, we went to drink wine in the arbor around which, at Toby's suggestion, there had been laid a low wall of old brick acquired from a Connecticut supplier specializing in scavenged materials. The missing element, I realized when we sat down, had to be Charlie's perennial air of imperiousness and triumph. He was more like everybody else, except of course for his size and strength which was ever more astonishing.

I have come to talk to you about Toby. Thanks to your confidence in him, your generosity, and, I suppose, the medication, he had a good summer. Now the honeymoon is over. He feels diminished. What a dreadful expression! Never mind, I've used it. Naturally, he doesn't want his weakness to show; he is very sensitive about it. So much pride, his and mine! Offense taken at trifles. That's why I am allowing this evening's preposterous celebration to take place. He didn't want people to say it had been canceled on his account. As though I cared! I thought you should know this before you meet.

Is it bad?

Yes—probably. Of course, his doctor is doing all the right things.

I am very sorry.

As I imagined the void that had opened before him, the embarrassment that overcame me was at least as strong as my feeling of pity. Together, they prevented me from finding a more adequate expression for sympathy or desire to help, and yet made silence intolerable. Instinctive garrulousness prevailed, so that hastily I told him of the importance to the Chinese, and others, like the Japanese and Koreans, whose cultures derived from China, of the sixtieth birthday, the figure sixty being the product of multiplying twelve (the number of animals each of which characterizes a year in the Chinese calendar) by five (the number of variable qualities of man). Thus sixty signifies the completion of a life cycle and the birthday marks the beginning of the period of "luck and age." I told him that, according to tradition, rich men have a duty to make presents of gold pieces and finest fabrics, silk or cashmere, to members of their households.

Toby was right to insist that you give the party, I concluded, it's a grand birthday.

I was launching into a disquisition on Chinese views about properties of numbers that made them lucky or unlucky when he interrupted me.

Perhaps in China; not here and not for me. For me, it's the first of the Stations of the Cross.

He looked at his watch, stared at me for a moment, and said, Come upstairs to that cocotte's bathroom you had Toby build for you. I want to show you something.

Not without apprehension, I followed. The new bathroom was, in fact, striking. We had enlarged it so that, for the first time in my life, I was the master of a dressing room. Toby had had the insides of the closets lined with sandalwood, the doors were full-length mirrors, and a daybed covered with chintz portraying birds of the Amazon jungle stood at an oblique angle to the window. I was to rest upon it, wrapped in towels, after my bath.

Charlie was never without a jacket in the country, inside his house or out. For the evening, these were apt to be voluminous, double-breasted blazers of heavy, smooth wool. During the day, he gave preference to tweed creations, the weight and roughness of which suited the season and the activity he had undertaken (thornproof, for instance, when he walked in the Billington woods) or, as now, at the height of the summer's heat, unlined silk. He railed against my habit of going about in shirtsleeves, wallet sticking out of the back pocket of my trousers, according to him like a sailor on leave who has been invited to spend the weekend with somebody's aunt. I watched him kick off his loafers and, more deliberately, remove his jacket, shirt, and trousers, until arms akimbo, majestic and naked, he stood in front of one of my mirrors. I noted that he wore no underpants.

Draw near, he said. Do not be afraid, you little devil. This isn't a pass. It will be a demonstration of the physiology of aging.

First, my face. You will have observed that I have turned gray—in that respect it helps to have once been blond. The color change is less unpleasant. Of course, my hair has remained thick. A tonsure will not needlessly inform the laity of my tastes. That is because my hair, like my mother's, is so surprisingly wiry. We used to wonder about the purity of the race, down there in Virginia. Speaking of what's wiry, behold my eyebrows. They have been invaded by pubic hair. Therefore, I pluck them. Each morning, I remove the more indecent hairs, those that curl, push in previously unaccustomed directions, or show split ends. It's a losing battle; their successors are even more *voyants*. Other pubic hairs protrude from inside my nose, itself thickened and bulbous—perhaps because, in defiance of my sainted mother's injunctions, I have always picked it. Soon its tip will be indistinguishable in form and jocund color from the gland that finishes my dick. Eyes injected with blood, the right one unpleasantly rheumy. Under these eyes, the windows of my soul, puckered brown bags, with striations and folds like a scrotum, studded with little warts. Brow permanently furrowed. Thus Priapus has usurped the place of Mars. Two years ago, before we knew of his sorrows—you realize now that he has become the man of sorrows—Toby wanted me to have these bags surgically reduced. Stretched and then sewed up from inside the lids, I suppose. Why? Was he ashamed of my aspect? A rare movement toward sadism and mutilation? Of course, I refused. Now it must be too late for the knife, and even if it weren't, and I should, *contra naturam*, consent to such a procedure, what would Toby think? That my new, gay eyes are a get-well gift to him, or the lure I was preparing for another young fellow?

Give me your hand.

I held it out. He opened my palm and passed it over his breasts, under his armpits, and down toward his belly.

That's right, he said, relax and avoid excitement. I have always thought there was a fruit inside you, but this is not your day. Don't think of sex, feel my skin and all these frigging bumps. More warts, growing ecstatically like weeds. Fear death by cancer. That is my opinion, as yet unconfirmed by my doctor. Can't say I would care about his opinion were he to have one. For now, I scratch at the little bastards until they bleed. Like this! I also examine myself for the big ones with oddly shaped edges, black harbingers of disaster.

Using a thick yellow fingernail he scooped bits of flesh from his stomach and made a stain of blood on the mirror, as though he were preparing a laboratory smear.

Do I disgust you? Bear with me, I don't think we will need a stool sample today.

He cradled his penis in one hand and testicles in the other.

Nothing much to report here. Slowness, occasional dysfunction, inevitable retreat of libido. Only remedy is promiscuity—the old call: change partners and do-si-do! My skin, especially on the legs, deserves your attention. It's thin like rice paper. Inside my trousers and socks, when I wear them, it peels, leaving a fine white snow like dandruff! These are, my dear Max, extravagant disorders, not autumn's rich increase. I have gone to seed, like you, like that superannuated rhubarb plant under your window. The ghoulish shame of it is that I am as strong as that rhubarb, indestructible. How many times have you tried to kill it and failed?

The truth is I haven't. I rather like it. It's practically the only thing that was planted by me.

Quite in character. One who has power to hurt and will do none. If I have revealed to you more than to any human being, it is because you have not used my words against me or in your own cause.

While he put on his clothes I wiped the stain off the mirror. We went downstairs. He refused my offer of another glass of wine.

Toby is waiting with lunch. I want him to eat his meals, he said.

He had come on his racing bicycle and refused also my offer to put it in the trunk of my car and drive him to the other side of the valley. I walked alongside him to the end of the gravel driveway. There he fastened his trouser legs with rubber bands, mounted the bicycle, and pedaled off at great speed.

MY FATHER WAS almost twenty years older than my mother. She had been his student. He died when I was in my last year of boarding school. His retirement coincided with an illness from which he never recovered. It absorbed most of his and my mother's attention. Our kitchen shelves were filled with special foods, all of them repellent, corresponding to his ever-changing diet. Leftovers cooked with margarine, in dishes covered with saucers and later in plastic containers, unfinished bottles of strange oils, and watery cottage cheese littered the refrigerator. I recoiled at their sight. On the windowsills in the kitchen, as well as in the bathroom that I shared with them, were his pills and, in larger bottles, the potions he ingested before and after meals, while he ate, upon arising, and at bedtime. The apparatus my mother used to give him enemas hung from a hook on the bathroom door, under his pajamas. As the number of household chores he felt unable to perform grew, he took to preparing, in anticipation of my visits on school holidays, a list of tasks he had saved up for me. The list would be presented sometimes before I had even crossed the threshold, at the bus stop where he met me in his Nash. Washing that car and simonizing it were among them. He ended in a Providence hospital, permanently catheterized, other tubes conducting yellowish liquids to his body connected to machines that surrounded his bed like unknown relatives. In comparison, my mother's exit, four years later, seemed triumphant. She fell down the cellar stairs, headfirst, arms and legs splayed. I like to think she never recovered her consciousness.

As I dressed for Charlie's party, and then drove to his house in the last of the sunset, I thought about that hospital room, the sore at the corner of my father's mouth where the tube leading to his esophagus had rubbed against the lip, and the mixture of patience and eagerness with which he greeted each new procedure. He was lucid and wrote orders, imprecations, and answers to the occasional question on a pad of paper within reach of his right hand. There was no doubt that he wanted the cure to continue. Why? I would ask his doctor. I had always known my father as a valetudinarian, he was certainly very cautious, but I had never had reason before to think that he was a coward. Why had he this insane reluctance to die?

It's the fear of final impotence, total and irreversible, the end to all knowledge, he told me. Only people who die suddenly avoid it.

Ricky and Edwina Howe, the van Lenneps, the gay cellist performing at Tanglewood, and I represented the Berkshires. Most of the guests were from the world of Charlie's other affections, perhaps more permanent, and in the years since I had become a part of his retinue I had come to know them sufficiently well for exclamations that served as greetings, embraces, and kisses. Among them were several architects of a renown that at least they considered equal to Charlie's and a family of real estate developers with a well-publicized devotion to culture; the most worldly among critics of architecture and art, and a giant of a man who had recently acquired the magazines they wrote for; the head of

an investment bank for whom Charlie had constructed a
mansion of celebrated opulence on many acres of East
Hampton waterfront (the last such work, he claimed, he
would undertake); a marquess in whose Venetian palace
Charlie willingly sojourned; gorgeously colorful among the
black of these figures, big-game wives or companions, and
the divorcées whose souls and amatory affairs Charlie was
directing, in part because he genuinely liked the company of
women and in part because, in principle, he preferred his
table to be balanced, even though this was a goal he seldom
achieved. The invitation had specified cocktails at eight and
carriages at a quarter after eleven. Their automobiles lined
the road—on aesthetic grounds, Charlie did not tolerate the
presence of cars near his house. Before they turned into
pumpkins, these guests would be hurtling down the Taconic
on their way back to New York. Charlie's indifference to the
comfort of others and his hauteur were greater than the
Howes'. He would not have taken the trouble, I was willing
to bet, to look for lodgings anywhere nearby for this crew of
revelers. The absence of younger members of the cama-
rilla—a designer working for Charlie, and a photographer
and an actor who were a couple—surprised me; they were
Toby's age, and I had expected to see them at the party for
his sake, if not for Charlie's.

I looked for Toby and found him in the smaller living
room, before the fire. He was thinner than when I saw him
last and had a small Band-Aid above his upper lip. Like my father's, I thought. There was another one on his cheek. I
kissed him, although this had not been my habit, and told
him I was very grateful for his work. The house was just as I

had hoped; would he come to see the finished product and witness the owner's admiration?

Perhaps tomorrow afternoon. Are you heating your pool? I might have a swim. You wouldn't mind?

The water will be at room temperature. Come to lunch first, with Charlie, and bring some cheese if there is any left. You can swim afterward.

We agreed on that plan. I told him about Rodney Joyce's lawsuit against his new Saudi neighbor across the lake who had taken to waterskiing in front of the Rumorosa and the letters of insult they had exchanged.

He is a fat prince, I said, with a little beard and bodyguards who have longer beards and guns as well and follow in a bigger boat when His Highness is on skis. Edna thinks they will dynamite the dock or drive a car bomb up to the veranda.

That's Lebanese stuff. According to my father, Saudis are wimps.

Some wimps! That must be when they aren't lapidating adulterers or cutting off the hands and feet of pickpockets! I have been told by a friend who lived there—I think in Jidda—that on Fridays adulterers are sewed in burlap bags up to the neck and then released in a public place. They waddle around like ducks. The authorities prepare neat piles of fist-sized rocks for the occasion, from which the faithful help themselves and start stoning!

He stared at me. I think that stopped a while ago.

Perhaps, but they were still at it in the sixties, I insisted. My friend, a very precise person, said he would first go to the barber to get a shave and then watch the executions. Saudis also like floggings. Then there is their fixation on hawking.

Training hawks is a very cruel process. The eyelids of young birds are stitched closed, to make them blind, and therefore dependent on their owner. Then, when the bird's dependency is judged sufficient, they cut the stitches open and real instruction begins.

Toby covered his eyes with his hands and turned away from me.

Stop, he said. I don't want to think of these things. I guess the old man was joking or was wrong.

More likely he was only thinking of Saudis he meets in the casino!

Toby didn't reply. From the other room, Charlie was calling us to the table. I brought myself to ask the question I had been avoiding.

How do you really feel?

He smiled. Pretty bad—or good. Depends on the day, and what you compare it with. But I'll be all right.

I was seated next to Edwina Howe, whose rank if not age had given her the place of honor next to Charlie. On my own right was Toby. This was something of a surprise. I had, in fact, completely forgiven Toby such injury as there was to forgive, but how were he and Charlie to know it? It was tempting to conclude that their natures were trusting, in a way that mine was not. On the other hand, it was equally possible that they had not thought about my feelings, or were indifferent to them.

Edwina wore one of her habitual embroidered silk sheaths—associated in my mind with old photographs of Madame Chiang Kai-shek—that would have been a challenge to a woman half her years, but in fact revealed a shape at once trim and feminine. At seventy or more, Edwina had a bosom that was, as she might have said, *sortable*! Over beautifully stretched skin, she was made up as though to appear on stage; necklaces, bracelets, rings, and earrings of striking colors and great complexity were displayed from her neck plunging into her décolletage, on her wrists and fingers, and from her ears. "Howe paste" was Edwina's name for her jewelry, as if to forestall any question about the provenance and nature of these cunning garnitures and, incidentally, to underline her disarming simplicity. The merest hint of an emerald tiara perched in her thinning but still quite red and well-organized hair. I wondered whether she entrusted the curling of this endangered part of her charms to a Lenox operator or had found Charlie's birthday worth a rapid trip to New York.

Toby had turned his back on me to talk to a journalist. Edwina was in conversation with Charlie. Across the table, voices were raised in a debate about Pete Rose's exclusion from baseball. Bart Giamatti had died the previous day, only one week after that decision was made. Was there a causal link between the two events? Had the heart attack been brought on by the stress the controversy had generated, or was it retribution for what Giamatti had done to Rose? The latter suggestion was shouted down: there had been no vendetta, the suggestion one might be "punished" by an illness was barbaric. Someone interjected: How about cholesterol and cigarettes? The publishing magnate wanted my opinion on whether Rose had had the benefit of due process. I answered, truthfully, that as I didn't follow the game I had paid little attention to the proceedings. My answer was received with the scorn I had anticipated. I raised the ante: the only aspect of the Giamatti affair that had interested me was his decision, after he had resigned as president of Yale, to enter professional baseball.

Go back to the rule against perpetuities, you wet macaroon, boomed Charlie. That was the whole point of his departure. He wanted to run baseball!

Doubtless, I would have been remitted to my black hole if Charlie, now aroused about baseball, had not abruptly abandoned Edwina. We had not seen each other since my divorce. Without missing a beat she spoke to me.

We are so sorry about Camilla. It was lovely, especially for Ricky, to have her as a neighbor, and so unexpected!

I acquiesced.

You too, of course! Although we haven't seen you nearly enough. Lawyers work too hard, even during their holidays. Dean always did. I am certain Foster did too, when he was in practice. But they always found time to be charming to everybody! Don't you agree?

If you mean Dean Acheson and John Foster Dulles, I can't tell. I didn't know them.

What a pity! You would have liked them so much. Dean, especially, was always kind to young people. Such a tragedy!

You mean that Dulles turned out to be Acheson's successor?

Young people today; that poor Toby.

She had not lowered her voice. Reflexively, I looked over my shoulder.

She reproved me: People never hear what's said about them except if one whispers. You mustn't allow yourself to be too busy to help out here. Charlie's patience won't last. I have known him for such a long time.

So have I.

There, then you understand. His kindness is skin-deep. We leave in two weeks, unfortunately.

Really.

She reviewed their travel plans for me. The inference to be drawn was that, if a large number of important people were not at risk of being seriously inconvenienced by a change in the program, she and Ricky might have stayed to succor Toby themselves.

Soon after I met them, Camilla had explained to me the Howes' modus operandi. It had its roots in the high rate of English income tax, which led Ricky to choose Bermuda for his residence; Billington was out of the question, as it would have subjected Ricky's personal fortune to American tax. The advent of Ronald Reagan and Mrs. Thatcher had changed the arithmetic, but not the noble couple's habits. No longer accustomed to living under their own roof, except in the Berkshires, they had become highly adapted no-mads—regular guests in the houses of the more sedentary rich—with patterns of migration as regular as those of certain birds Rick studied. In late September, they could be spotted at the house of an Oriental prince in Paris, subsequently, toward Christmas, on a commodity store magnate's estate in Florida, then on a Central American island refuge of a family that owned the adjoining country, et cetera. This was an ecosystem of great delicacy. I sympathized with Edwina's unwillingness to disturb it.

I will leave our addresses and telephone numbers, she promised. It would be dreadful to be without news.

The effect of Charlie's habit of eating slowly, his imperturbable disregard of the empty plates of guests who had already been served twice, and the incompetence of the servers he had imported from Pittsfield was cumulative. We drank a heavy Italian red. Neither Charlie nor Ricky, who presided at the other end, paid attention to the general flow of the conversation. My attempt to attract Toby's attention failed. I realized that unless I rose to make a toast I was in Edwina's thrall for the rest of the evening—Charlie did not like leaving the table for coffee. It was my intention to make a toast, but I doubted that I had the right to go first. There were other people present whose initiative Charlie would find more flattering.

Meanwhile, Edwina returned to the subject of Camilla.

You do know that she is about to marry Roland?

No. Really?

Except for his age it does seem rather natural. They have always been so close. She has a good job and a little money of her own, and that will be a big help. Just as well the two of you didn't have any children. Is it because you can't?

I don't know. I am not sure that I ever had an opportunity to find out.

Ricky can't. So many men seem to be like that, but it's women who get the blame!

The news about Camilla and Roland hurt, although, of course, it didn't matter whether she married him or another. I was about to make my toast, after all, without having thought out what I would say, when Toby turned to me and whispered, Please help me get upstairs. I am not well.

A sort of bashfulness reinforced by its opposite, suppressed unhealthy curiosity, had previously confined me to the ground floor of Charlie's house. I had seen his bedroom only once, when he invited me to view the recently inherited Sargent portrait of a great-aunt he had installed there. On that occasion, I had also noted and admired his sculpted, blond art nouveau suite of furniture, particularly the bed, which recalled a giant seashell over which peeked smirking mermaids. It was large enough for two. Did Toby share it? Did he and Charlie lounge on the panther skins thrown over that aquatic couch? Leaning against me as I supported him with both arms, whimpering very softly, Toby said, No, not here, when I instinctively turned at the top of the stairs in the direction of Charlie's room. It's on the other side, at the end of the corridor.

This room was huge too, directly over the back flower garden. Unless this Victorian house had been built with two master bedrooms, they had surely added to Toby's room an adjoining guest room. I deposited Toby in an armchair and asked what the matter was, what I should do to help.

It's my eyes. Like black spots before me. I'm scared.

Are you fainting? Do you want a cold compress?

No, I'm so scared. I think I'm going blind.

I helped him climb on the bed and put pillows behind his back. All the while, he kept on making his little crying noises. I said I would leave him for just a moment, to get Charlie.

Don't, not now. Maybe you should. Turn on the television. I want to be able to look.

A baseball diamond filled the screen.

Is that better?

I can see. It's just these whirs that don't stop.

I stood at the dining room door. Dick Moses was working his way through a sort of catalogue raisonné of Charlie's buildings, publications, and medals. Just as I thought the end had been reached, he meandered back to their days together at the School of Design. There had been a joint project for a library, which a now-forgotten chairman of the jury had had the temerity to criticize before the class as "weakly derivative." Like all your work! was Charlie's loud rejoinder. During Moses's description of the ensuing pandemonium, and the clinking of glasses around the dinner table, I made my way to Charlie and said, loud enough to be heard by Edwina and the press magnate, Come upstairs for a moment, there's a call for you from Tokyo. It's some incomprehensible man whose name I didn't catch. Perhaps he wants to wish you happy birthday. Toby answered and is trying to keep him on the line.

At the foot of the stairs, I told him what had happened, and returned to my place next to Edwina. My glass was empty. Feigning distraction, I drank Edwina's, although Toby's was full as well.

How extraordinary that you boys heard the telephone ring! I was so engrossed by our conversation, my dear Max. You really must come to lunch just with Ricky and me. One is always interrupted at large parties.

It's Toby's own line. I guess he is used to listening for it.

That dear child! He stayed upstairs to share in Charlie's joy!

Minutes passed. Majestic and grim, Charlie entered the room. His voice filled it.

Your carriages are waiting. What I must do upstairs will keep me for a while. And he raised his arms, palms open, as though to bless the congregation.

I did not follow the others. Pretending to look for a book in the living room—although in fact I was sure that no one paid attention to me—I waited until the last guest was out the door and then went back upstairs to Toby's room. Just as I had left him, immobile, he was staring at a commercial for small Ford trucks. Perhaps the game had ended. Only now he was weeping, his face was wet with tears, and he was doing nothing to dry them. Unintelligible, Charlie could be heard over the jingle from somewhere down the hall. He slammed down the receiver and came into the room.

Aha, you're still here. Little Miss Discretion. No, forgive me. It's just as well you lied. They're mostly like me: cold, insincere people, barely polite enough to hide it. Get Toby into other clothes, something warm, while I also change. We will start for New York. The doctor wants to put him on some drug.

Will you call me?

He did, a few days later, after I had returned to Cambridge and my teaching. It was a neurological problem, he told me, more frightening than serious. Toby was already back at Pratt. He, Charlie, was going to Europe, Düsseldorf principally, to keep promises he had made when the city engaged him to build the new lyric arts theater. Was I planning to be away? No? That's what he had thought, so he counted on me to look a bit after Toby. Wasn't it strange how the world revolved? Even in Beijing he had felt there was a link between the boy and me, a dependency of a younger brother on his elder. Very beautiful, really. I might want to come to New York on some weekends. Otherwise, his driver was available; he would bring Toby to me—Billington or Cambridge, it didn't matter. That would tide Toby over until he felt confident enough of his vision to drive a car.

And when will you return?

Certainly by Thanksgiving. I can always fly back for a few days if there is a problem.

THAT OLD WITCH, Edwina, had been at least half-right, though I refrained from writing to her about my new duties or any other aspect of the situation. She had a network of other informants, I imagined, busy on the telephone from messy lukewarm beds after the tisane, toast, and stock tables. We settled into a routine, the boy and I. After the hospital, where they stopped the black spots, he did not go back to his apartment. A friend, possibly a fellow student, moved in—to water plants, clean the aquarium, and discourage burglars from entering through the skylight. Toby had refused to have bars placed over it, claiming they would make him feel he was imprisoned in a small Max Ernst. He lived instead at Charlie's. When I came to see him on weekends, in the city, I declined the use of the vaunted guest quarters of the River House apartment and stayed instead at the Peninsula—convenient, pompously refurbished, and half-empty, having in common with the sparkling white establishment in Kowloon only the name and occasional clumps of Hong Kong Chinese guests, done up in suede, waiting for their stretch limos to pull up—and, as he was still rather shaken and tired easily, first thing in the morning I would walk eastward to the river, the half mile I covered giving me the impression that I was managing to combine attention to my own health with watching over Toby's. We sat together in the study. Either he managed to get his schoolwork done during the week, or his interest in it was waning. Huddled in the corner of the couch, an alpaca plaid over his shoulders, the TV volume turned down, so as to let me get on with my reading and occasional note taking, he absorbed what the pundits were saying of that month's clownish and premonitory events. Then during lunch he would comment on Cardinal Glemp, like some transvestite Joan of Arc, emerging as the champion of the nuns of Auschwitz, the navy's glee at having found the perfect scapegoat—a "loner" (therefore gay, not one of us) and already dead—to blame for the humiliation of the *Iowa*, and Ed Koch and the Evil Empire unraveling in unison. These were companionable meals, served by Charlie's houseman. I made a point of disregarding the pills he set out for Toby. The intrusive memories of how my father ate, awakened somehow by the diet additives Toby was consuming, were harder to keep at bay.

In October, he told me that, if he was driven up and then back to the city, he could manage Billington. The leaves had just turned scarlet and ruby. I moved the television set into my guest room, and it was there, he in bed and I on the chaise longue he arranged to have upholstered for me with bottle-green cut velvet, that we celebrated the New York Stock Exchange's free fall on Friday, October 13. I say that without irony, as my State Street trustees had turned every stock that was not "our bank's" into cash some weeks earlier. While I drank my bourbon—Toby had problems with his mouth or gums that made drinking even wine painful—I meditated on the possibility of urging them to go quickly back into the market, which suddenly seemed full of bargains. Were the black orphans and I on the road to even greater prosperity?

In fact, I found the onslaughts and retreats of Toby's sores—most often on his face, hands, and forearms—embarrassing and scary. The former, because they were so insistently visible, and yet I never alluded to them; the latter, because they told me he was not making a recovery. When I was in Cambridge, there operated, parallel to Toby's attendance at classes, a system of visits to his doctor (perhaps he saw more than one) and treatments, the nature of which I only surmised. That was the circle within which those eruptions were dealt with. My not wanting to know more than that was a mixture of respect for Toby's dignity, squeamishness about illness, and fear of reaching that point where pity intersects with contempt.

I thought that Toby read me like an open book but did not take offense. Perhaps he preferred silence; I could not be sure. But did I have the right to observe in silence? Had I not assumed some sort of responsibility for how he was cared for? The law of torts is full of horror stories of Good Samaritans undertaking to be helpful to a man bleeding by the roadside, botching the job, and being held liable in damages. In moral terms, was that my case? On the telephone, Charlie's reassurances were invariable: Toby had the best doctor in the country; he, Charlie, spoke with Toby daily and once a week with the doctor; if anything needed to be done, the doctor would tell him at once. What did that mean?

We were watching euphoric lunar figures gesticulating and embracing one another, some astride the Berlin Wall. Toby, as usual, was on the bed, covered by a light blanket. I had pulled up a chair to be near. In a moment of abandon, I slapped him on the knee. He could not restrain a howl of pain. Moments later, seeing how upset I was, he managed a grin and showed me his leg. It was covered by what looked like leeches but, in reality, were hot, black, suppurating scabs.

Some days later, Charlie returned, full of stories about the spring of nations. My watch was over. The following week he telephoned again. Toby had had a transfusion, with immediate, almost miraculous, effect. Would I come to celebrate at Thanksgiving lunch in New York? I said that was not possible: I was planning a private celebration with Laura. We had been conducting a very old-fashioned courtship, writing letters each day, sometimes more often. At last, she had agreed to marry me; she was coming to Cambridge, to Bluebeard's castle, for a long visit.

HAPPINESS: it is made of Laura's voice. She gossips with her sister in Florence; she teases and laughs; the conversa-

tions are interminable; they call each other as soon as Laura
awakens, at the end of the afternoon, and also at any time of
the day if something that strikes one or the other as funny
has happened; they have the sense of humor of nine-year-
olds playing hopscotch. When I come home from Langdell, I
am greeted by that enchanting recitative. She sings and
hums in her bath, and when she irons rapidly, just as we are
about to go out, one of those silk jackets that are indispensable to her wardrobe (she likes to thrust her hands into their
pockets, her fingers are unbearably long, like a magician's, I
do not tire of watching them and I am grateful that they are
bare of rings), while driving my car as though we were on an
autostrada, and on our walks along the Charles. Her reper-
tory of children's songs is endless. She likes to hold my hand.

Comfortable on the window seat, she reads in the white
winter sun. Plain, serviceable glasses have settled on the tip
of her serious nose. Now that she will be my wife I am allowed to see them. Before, she faked it; they were always
tinted, like a movie star's. Her legs—they too are long and
end in big, sturdy feet, like a Manchu woman's, of which she
is very proud—are draped over the arm of her chair or
stretch out before her, modestly crossed at the ankles. The
butcher and the greengrocer are her acolytes. I have known
these men for almost thirty years, and now they snub me. At
her command, fat gray sausages appear miraculously in the
bollito misto. My students interest her; it doesn't matter if I
invite them at the last minute. She will throw another fistful
or two of pasta into the water that boils in the smallest and
tinniest of pots—bought by her, because mine, heavy and

enameled, are too fancy. She seeks their views on President Bush, abortion rights, and the strange case of Jim and Tammy Bakker. They call her Laura; by tacit agreement, I remain Professor Strong. St. Thomas held that when a powerful emotion seizes a man's faculties it displaces all others. There is no room in my heart, mind, or life for anyone but Laura.

In the beginning of January, there comes an angry storm. I put on high rubber boots and walk to the Law School, then telephone her when I am ready to return for lunch. She tells me we will meet halfway. Brattle Street is deserted. Finally, her silhouette, tall and gracious, appears in the swirling whiteness. She takes my arm. No hat. Huge, wet snowflakes stick to her hair and eyelashes. Quick, we must hurry. Everywhere in the house there are yellow tulips and anemones of all colors, some in vases I have never seen. How mad, how splendid to have looked for them in this weather. It was essential, she answers—I wanted you to know right away that I am very happy. I put my arms around her. Very cold and wet cheeks and nose; she hasn't dried them. As I hold her, she whispers into my ear that a miracle has happened. She is pregnant!

A FEW DAYS LATER, Laura left for Milan. A fellow dealer wanted to bid for her gallery; she was in a hurry to wind up her business in Italy. As though startled from a dream, I heard Charlie's voice on the telephone. He had reached me at home, late in the evening. What was my blood type? I consulted my dog tags, preserved in a file folder together with my sharpshooter medals and a group photograph of my platoon. It was the same as Toby's. Yes, I would come to New York for the weekend and give as much blood as was allowed within the span of three days.

He was in an upstairs bedroom in Charlie's apartment, on a hospital bed, feet elevated. I recognized the alpaca plaid. There were silk shades with silk tassels on the sconces and table lamps. The light was mauve. He had insisted on seeing me, but I was to be careful not to tire him, as this was not a good day, and to make no reference to the bed or the oxygen tank.

Death is the greatest of sculptors. His modeling knife had removed all but the most indispensable matter from Toby's face, indenting the cheeks and lengthening and refining the nose, until it had taken the form of a coin made of yellow and gray alabaster. His eyes looked at me from arched spaces, like Romanesque crypts, of prodigious depth; one did not think there could be room for them in the skull. But the eyes themselves were clear and luminous, and so gentle that I thought that all that was good in Toby had been concentrated in them. He made a croaking sound when he greeted me, causing the nurse—a pink young woman I had not noticed so long as she had remained in a chair in the corner of the room—to crank him up to a sitting position, offer a glass of milk, and put Vaseline on his lips. He thanked her and said that was much better. Indeed, she had almost succeeded in giving him back his normal voice. I told him about the baby.

It will be a Leo, he observed. Like me.

That's right, and when it's baptized we will ask you to be the godfather! Perhaps both you and Arthur, if he is willing to agree to look after the kid's religious upbringing.

Two godfathers like that! The child will be sure to grow up to do something bad.

After a while he held out his hand to me. It was a very slow gesture.

I am glad they are going to fill me up with your blood. Charlie also has the same type, so our three bloods are getting all mixed up together. I think that's a sign. Some part of both of you will remain inside me. We are blood brothers.

You've been watching too many Mafia movies!

The nurse had been listening.

We're all related like that, she said, only people don't take time to think about it.

VI

I STOPPED THE CAR as close as possible to the snow-
bank and got out. The pickup truck, which had tailgated
me ever since I entered the village, stopped also, just
ahead. The chains on its wheels ground violently, sending a
shower of mud. The driver rolled down his window and
yelled. He had wispy yellow hair, yellow aviator glasses, and
a thin nose set in the sort of delicate, old-fashioned face not
uncommon among inhabitants of certain remote Berkshire
villages. The words were surely insults, but I couldn't make
them out or understand the reason for his rage. I shook my
head in a gesture of incomprehension and walked in the direction of the mourners trudging past the church and along
the path uphill to the old cemetery. The cab door slammed.
In a moment he was beside me. In his hand was an ax handle.

Fucking queer, he cried, asshole, you fucking crawl on the
highway. I should have run your fucking ass off the road.

I am sorry I held you up. My car was skidding.

And then, without a logical connection, I added, This is
the funeral of a friend.

Up your ass.

He spat a glob of phlegm like an eyeball on the snow,

directly at my feet. I wondered if he was about to hit me. Instead, he gave me the finger and headed back toward the road. I heard him slam the door of his truck again, then the motor being raced and the clatter of chains.

The snow had been melting all week. There was still a thick crust of it on the ground, but the tombstones were bare, even the horizontal ones scattered among the pines like counters for a game played by the hand of a giant. A yellow tractor with a scoop attached to its front end stood near the hole they had made for Toby. Around it, people were shaking hands and avoiding smiles. It seemed to me that they were also avoiding contact with the woman who was clearly Toby's mother. Rouged, her silver hair set in a permanent under a black toque, she was in a wheelchair. A female keeper and a man who looked like the driver of a rented limousine stood behind her. Around them, a void.

I approached, introduced myself, and said, How do you do. I am terribly sorry. I loved Toby.

She stared. Then her face relaxed and she held out her hand. Perhaps she thought that she had managed to recognize me.

I am very glad to see you. Isn't it lovely here?

In deference to a look from the keeper, I bowed and withdrew. That the mother would be brought out for the occasion had not occurred to me, but who was to say that Charlie had not done the right thing even if, as Toby maintained, she understood nothing? Otherwise, I could see that the usual suspects had been assembled: representative elders from Stockbridge and Lenox, Edwina and Ricky, their suntans like airline luggage tags proving they had come directly from

Florida, certain faces I had seen at Charlie's birthday dinner. Glowering, squeezed into a heavy double-breasted black greatcoat, in his left hand pearl gray gloves and a black homburg, he received new arrivals at the side of the lady minister. I was crushed in his vast embrace.

Instinctively, we formed a semicircle facing them. The keeper pushed the wheelchair into the center. Charlie nodded approval.

Thanks to you all. Toby's mother and I are deeply honored by your presence. Please do not expect speeches or refreshments. After the entombment, we will scatter like fallen leaves—in silence.

The minister read from a thin, worn-out book. Unable to concentrate on the familiar words, I studied her appearance. What was the significance of the color of her stole? Was it for funerals, or did it indicate rank in the church? Under her surplice one could see a brown fur coat. It was beaver, I supposed, just as perfect for the climate and this outdoor function as her laced boots of beige and white shorthaired hide, rather like what one used to see in pictures of Eskimo families standing outside an igloo.

At last, she closed her book. Some men with shovels moved forward. Charlie raised his hand to stop them, whereupon I noticed standing alone, beside a fir tree, a short gent, dressed in black like Charlie, but with a long English undergraduate's scarf, red with odd cream stripes, wrapped around his neck. He moved forward, halted, and began to sing. A virile, very dark voice spread over the hillside. It was huge enough to fill even the emptiness above.

It dawned on me that this must be the great Italian

tenor—the best, some claimed, since Caruso—who had recently moved into nearby South Egremont. I knew the music: it was from Verdi's *Requiem*, the great solo wherein the trembling soul pleads for salvation.

Later that day, I looked up the text. For once, it was in the right place, inside the compact disc cover. As I read it,

Ingemisco tanquam reus,
Culpa rubet vultus meus,
Supplicanti parce Deus.

Qui Mariam absolvisti
Et latronum exaudisti
Mihi quoque spem dedisti.

Preces meae non sunt dignae,
Sed tu bonus fac benigne,
Ne perenni cremer igne.

Inter oves locum praesta
Et ab haedis me sequestra
Statuens in parte dextra.

I groan like a criminal:
Guilt turns my face red,
God, spare Thy supplicant.

Thou hast absolved Mary
And granted the thief's prayer,
Give me also hope.

My prayers are not worthy,
But Thou art good, so prove kind
Lest I burn in eternal fire.

Give me a place among the sheep,
Keep me away from the goats,
Adjudge me a place on the right.

my astonishment at the audacity—or was it cruelty—of
Charlie's farewell to Toby grew, until it turned into something like awe.

It was, of course, possible that the choice had not been his,
that the distinguished performer, ordinarily far too grand for
this kind of engagement yet apparently willing to be of service to Charlie, had told him that here was something suitable, and of the right length, that he could sing in the open
air without accompaniment, and that Charlie, in his disarray
and grief, agreed without question. But I rejected that explanation. Charlie was too deliberate in all matters of cere-
mony, too pedantic even about casual gestures, not to have
examined each word that was to be sung and its implica-
tions. Was it not more likely that he had decided, perhaps
long ago, to have this lament performed at his own funeral,
if not Toby's, that he knew its text as though it had been
etched on his flesh with acid? Indeed, if the great tenor happened to suggest its use, didn't Charlie take the coincidence
to be a hideous sign, an obscene wink signaling complicity
and agreement on a matter he surely preferred to keep to
himself? For what was the meaning of these words—so
humble, submissive, and, yes, saccharine—when applied to

Toby but mockery, a knife pointed at the heart? If Verdi was on Charlie's mind, he might as well have arranged for a baritone to sing Iago's *Credo in un Dio crudel*. The message would have been more obvious, but to my mind less perverse and harsh.

"I groan like a criminal." Yes, in a short life Toby had done his share of groaning—upon the discovery of his taste for men; when that taste first became apparent to others so that, at times, he was thankful for the dementia that had cut his mother off from knowledge; as the act was consummated, whether on Charlie's exquisite bed or in men's toilets in certain subway or railroad stations, while he leaned against a urinal; and with the revelation of each new facet of the disease. "Guilt turns my face red." What was the flush of pleasure, when it suffused Toby's face, but the guilty blush of shame, each of the gestures that brought the pleasure having been of old condemned as an abomination? "Adjudge me a place on the right." Would that Judge set Toby among the righteous? No. Since the first coupling, He had turned the male seed into an instrument of contamination, so that sin and death conjoined are fatally borne by the seed, however it is spilled, and are the true birthright of all who grow from the seed. And forgiveness? Perhaps for the thief, strung up beside the Cross on which the Son was nailed and stabbed. But that Son—or was it the Father?—who found it needful to absolve Mary, for the sole reason that she too had been born of the seed, would He take pity on a dead little faggot? On Toby the receptacle, Toby the penetrator, Toby the rag soaked with semen, Toby the goat? Yes, beg Him. *Fac benigne!* Be kind! Grant cherubic Toby, Toby the easy lay, a place among the cherubim! Not bloody likely. Isn't that what my proud, sardonic, sentimental, and self-hating friend Charlie would have said had he his wits about him?

And I, thinking of Laura's child and mine, and of what might lie ahead, agreed, and wished that the great voice had been a shriek, crying: Mourn, wretched mothers of sons not yet conceived! Mourn, wail and beat your breasts. Mourn, and beware! A lord of evil sends plagues to torment the living and infect even the unborn!

VII

H OO HOO, was it ever cold in the glen! Lambent
stalactites of ice, rivulets seized in the face of the
rock, crevices steel gray, blind mirrors framed by
briar and snow, reflecting nothing. Fleet of foot, I raced,
leaping from boulder to boulder, vaulting over tree trunks.
Limbs of huge oaks gave way; from the frozen earth, I tore
saplings with their roots, like tufts of grass, and cast them
into the turbid lower void. And always my war cry: Hoo hoo!
Abruptly, the day died. Hecate appeared out of the night,
denser in blackness than night herself, majestic. On her left
shoulder, she bore a moon. It was white like death. I hailed
her, fell on my knees, and groveled. I felt around me for the
place where the stones were sharpest, to beat my forehead
against them. I clawed at my face and lips. At last, I bled. I
licked and swallowed the blood, as I had swallowed him. Yellow crust, scabs, the taste of pus. Her moon leered at me. I
leapt in pursuit. Arrived above the tallest pines, where the
meadow like a shroud stretched toward the first star, I saw I
was alone. Boreal wind. Hoo it was cold! Stripped to the
waist, I cleansed the palms of my hands on gleaming snow,
which I dug from inside a deep mound, rubbed my eyes,

face, and breast with it. Only then, at last, I cupped my hands, carried fresh snow to my lips, and quenched my horrid thirst.

I descended through snowdrifts—strong as a bull, patient as an ox. From their balconies, leaning perilously, great constellations stared in wonder. Again, the tree line. There, brief slumber, like the touch of a god, purged me of all fever. Kyrie eleison! I raised my voice in a hymn of thanksgiving.

Charlie fell silent. He was still in black; evidently, he had not changed his clothes after the funeral. The black shoes he extended toward the embers in my fireplace were caked with mud. His eyes looked like raw meat. I had put a bottle of bourbon and the ice bucket on the low table next to his armchair. He refilled his glass and slept very quietly, with his mouth open. A few minutes later, he was awake. I supposed that he had been drinking all evening, long before he appeared, unexpected, at the door of my living room.

Oblige me, and do something about that miser's fire.

The handyman had sawed dead tree branches broken by the last storm into fireplace-sized pieces. Beside them he had stacked overgrown vines he had cleared. Overcoming my habitual fear of starting a chimney fire, I filled the fireplace to the brim. The flame surged like a wave. I went to the kitchen, found some hard biscuits and cheese, and set the food next to the bottle.

He ate attentively, licking his index and median fingers to pick up crumbs more easily from the plate. Some time passed in silence. He drained the remains of the bourbon into his glass and handed me the empty bottle.

You do have more? If not, scotch will be just fine.

I made another trip to the kitchen.

Good. Now throw in some real logs and sit down. There, these should be enough. Have a drink. Celebrate with me. I have done it, I have stepped off the ledge, it's over.

He poured some whiskey for me, put ice in it, refilled his own glass, and stared until I felt I must speak. It all seemed horribly clear, and I did not want to fall short of his candor. Therefore, I said to him, You mean you helped him commit suicide? It's awful that you had to do it, but surely it was the right thing.

Charlie laughed.

Suicide? Certainly not! Toby had no intention of killing himself. He wanted to hang in there. His own words! That's what he wanted. He was furious I had brought him here, and didn't stop complaining until I had promised to drive him back to the city the next day for another transfusion. Of course, we didn't make it. He died in the evening. He even made me telephone the nurses and tell them not to bother to come out. That's why he was alone.

I suppose you and Toby never discussed this point, he continued, so you don't know how strongly he felt that there should be a nice order of precedence in death. Like letting the older person go through the door first. *Après vous, Maman, après vous, Charlie.* I think the more elegant attitude in these circumstances might be: *Surtout, avant vous, Gaston!* There is only one argument to the contrary, which doesn't apply in my case, because I wasn't cut out to be a nurse, that Alphonse wants to stick around, Nurse Gaston, lave and bury him, and pay his bills. Subtleties of this sort were lost on Toby. All he knew was that he was dying and others weren't. His mother's having lost her marbles was a sort of mitigating circumstance, a partial excuse for her good physical health, but he really took it very hard that I had been, his word again, spared. Spared what? I would ask him. Your particular disease? You know nothing of how I will die, and why do you wish to be there to find out? Believe me, I would say, it's all quite random, who goes first and why and how, and quite immaterial. Take the massacre of the Innocents. Does it matter that there is no evidence to prove that a large number of the mothers impaled themselves on the Romans' swords or lost their minds from grief? Does it matter that mothers and fathers who saw their children butchered went right on doing their best to survive in Auschwitz, or Bergen-Belsen, or any other of those hell pits, and did in fact survive, and after the war raised new fucked-up families, just like everybody else? My foot! There is a famine in Ethiopia—pick any country in Africa. In one picture, a mother carries a withered child, in another it's some balloon on legs like hairpins playing in the dust, while momma and poppa are picked at by a bunch of birds. Are the living better off than the dead? Only the dead are spared, Toby, I would tell him. You have heard about the music of the spheres? It's the upgathered howl of pain, rising from every corner of the earth. Like a toilet bowl that has overflowed and yet some idiot keeps flushing. But I might as well have talked to a wall.

Without warning, he was asleep again. This time, he snored very loudly.

Aha, a good sign! I heard myself snore. Toby always claimed he could hear me from down the hall. Let no one say that Charlie Swan has murdered sleep!

He refused my offer of coffee.

Charlie, I said, have you been trying to say you killed Toby? If that's so, tell it to me, get it out of your mind, and don't talk about it again—I mean to anyone else. He was practically dead anyway. You only did what he should have asked of you.

Don't jump to conclusions, old friend. I don't need a lawyer, not this time. Toby died of what they call natural causes and, absent accident, so will I, to keep my part of the bargain. But if you like, I will a tale unfold. Just for you. Imagine my house. It's afternoon. Winter sunlight, a decent fire in the fireplace, irises and tulips arranged by me. I have fed Toby lunch. Custard brought from New York, chocolate milk, and pills. More pills—a stunning multitude—in little dishes cunningly displayed on my mother's night table, which I have moved into his room. But one night table is not enough. The rest of the pharmacy, a junkie's dowry of sedatives and tonics, occupies the cocktail tray I have placed on a trestle. Together with his poor treasures: photographs taken on a beach in Beirut, and I suppose at Christmas, held in a traveling wallet of cracked, faded leather that was his father's, the Easter egg with a clock inside it I gave him after our first night together, his loose-leaf address book, closed with a rubber band and bulging with business cards and scraps of paper crumpled like tissue. On them, the entire universe of a homeless waif. Heartbreak. What has he besides? The bed I let him use? His clothes? Pills and wads of sterile gauze?

I clear the dishes and come back. He is on the bed, propped up on the pillows, under that alpaca or mohair throw. I recall that I must have it cleaned. Face like the head of a dead sheep. I have brought very soft pajamas for him, to keep him warm—and to stop him from scratching his legs. Instead, he is wearing the antique woman's kimono embroidered with cranes I brought from Hong Kong. An effort at coquetry? Or does the silk feel better against his skin? In any case, the effect is grotesque. Cranes are a symbol of longevity. I wonder how much longer I can bear it, and sit down on a chair beside him.

You know, I can go to New York for the transfusion alone, he tells me. Mr. Babinski will drive me down, and once I'm in the city it's very easy. I'll call you if there is a problem.

At once, I begin to cry, and turn away quickly, so he won't see my face. It's all there, in those few words: his desperate will to continue—for what? Dependence. Fear of displeasing. Displeasing me. As though that were still an issue. And I said to myself that all I know, or think I know, about the human condition, everything I have so carefully explained to him—for one reason only, so that he would swallow enough of those goddamned pills and leave me at last in peace— missed the point. He wants fraternity, not equality. For a leper, real fraternity exists only with other lepers, not with the nice doctor from the Bronx who comes to look after him during a summer vacation. There is no fraternity between

the guy whose eyes have been seared by some Indian police-
man and the ladies and gentlemen of Amnesty. His brothers
are the guys in the same police station, the same prison, the
same cell, having the same plant juice dripped under their
eyelids.

And so I shift again in my chair, smile, and assure Toby
that it is in fact very convenient for me to be in New York for
a few days. I ask him to excuse me for a moment, I will be
right back.

I have always been proud of my teeth. If you haven't noticed before, look: they are white and perfect, as though I
had had them capped, but they are, in fact, entirely my own.
The only time my gums have bled is when I have been hit on
the mouth in the boxing ring. I take a metal fingernail file in
the bathroom and cut my gums savagely. Crisscross. Also the
insides of my cheeks. Then I go in to him. He has begun to
doze. I kneel down at the side of the bed, slide my hand
under that blanket. The kimono is already half-open. I caress
him, first at the ankles, moving up slowly, feeling for crusts
to avoid hurting the sores. For a while, he pretends I have not
waked him. Then his face lights up, eyes wide open. I hear
his breath. He thinks I want him, turns toward me, his thigh
lifts to meet my hand. He has been so very weak, I don't
know what to expect, but yes, it's ready. So I rise from my
knees, grab his waist, stoop, and take him. His stomach, his
buttocks, heave against my hands. A moment later, it has
been done, sealed! I linger like a bridegroom and let go gen-
tly, reluctantly. His fingers are in my hair, playing with my
ears. When he is quiet again, I show him the inside of my
mouth. From the taste, I can tell it is still bleeding. I look into

his eyes. For whatever it's worth, he knows that it will have to be the same for me.

Then I lie down beside him. He has turned on his side, with his back to me. The old spoon position, well known to bring comfort and peace. Except that, suddenly, it is not comfort I want. I pierce him. Like a battering ram. Without letting down my trousers. And all the while, the kid howls from pain.

The exigencies of my toilette. He too has composed himself and goes back to being grateful. I administer a sedative and show him where there are lots more should he want them. Then I say, I will leave the lights on in your room. I need a long walk now. Nothing more can happen to you until I return.

And I rush to that frozen glen. Hours later, I approach the house like a burglar. Leave the car on the road, creep quietly, quietly on the side of the driveway, so the gravel won't crunch. His light is still on.

He rinsed his mouth with the bourbon and winked at me. I managed to smile back. Some minutes passed. I heard what could be a muffled cry and ran upstairs. The bedroom door was open. In the wedge of light that came from the corridor I saw Laura's face. She was sleeping peacefully. I leaned my head against the door frame and remained there until my heart stopped pounding. She had lost a quantity of blood two days earlier, when she returned from Milan, but the doctor still hoped she would be able to keep the child.

When I came back downstairs, the room was empty. Dying coals glowed in the fireplace. The only glass on the coffee table was my own. Charlie had vanished.

I never have asked Charlie why he had that woman pray over the grave at Toby's funeral, or what was his reason for the Verdi lament. I suppose I was held back by a sort of shy respect. Much later, though, under different skies, as I turned the matter over in my mind, it occurred to me that Charlie might have laughed at my indignation had I told him about it. He had indeed come to look like an aged Mars. I could imagine him throwing back that gorgeous head and saying to me something like, My boy, I don't look at the ceiling of the Sistine Chapel to learn about paleontology. I haven't stopped praying because prayers aren't granted, any more than heterosexuals have stopped screwing because children are born to suffer and to die. I told the Wop to sing the *Requiem* because it's so beautiful.

A NOTE ON THE TYPE

This book was set in Monotype Dante, a typeface designed by Giovanni Mardersteig (1892–1977). Conceived as a private type for the Officina Bodoni at Verona, Italy, Dante was originally cut only for hand composition by Charles Malin, the famous Parisian punch cutter, between 1946 and 1952. Its first use was in an edition of Boccaccio's *Trattatello in laude di Dante* that appeared in 1954. The Monotype Corporation's version of Dante followed in 1957. Although modeled on the Aldine type used for Pietro Cardinal Bembo's treatise *De Ætna* in 1495, Dante is a thoroughly modern interpretation of that venerable face.

Printed and bound by
Arcata Graphics, Martinsburg, West Virginia
Designed by Peter A. Andersen